W9-CMP-008

THE PURLOINED PUZZLE

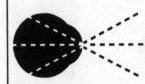

This Large Print Book carries the
Seal of Approval of N.A.V.H.

A PUZZLE LADY MYSTERY

THE PURLOINED PUZZLE

PARNELL HALL

THORNDIKE PRESS
A part of Gale, a Cengage Company

SOUTH HUNTINGTON PUB. LIB.
145 PIDGEGON HILL ROAD
HUNTINGTON STA., NY 11746

GALE
A Cengage Company

Farmington Hills, Mich • San Francisco • New York • Waterville, Maine
Meriden, Conn • Mason, Ohio • Chicago

Copyright © 2018 by Parnell Hall.
Thorndike Press, a part of Gale, a Cengage Company.

ALL RIGHTS RESERVED
This is a work of fiction. All of the characters, organizations, and events portrayed in this novel are either products of the author's imagination or are used fictitiously.
Thorndike Press® Large Print Mystery.
The text of this Large Print edition is unabridged.
Other aspects of the book may vary from the original edition.
Set in 16 pt. Plantin.

LIBRARY OF CONGRESS CIP DATA ON FILE.
CATALOGUING IN PUBLICATION FOR THIS BOOK
IS AVAILABLE FROM THE LIBRARY OF CONGRESS

ISBN-13: 978-1-4328-5395-2 (hardcover)

Published in 2018 by arrangement with Macmillan Publishing Group, LLC/St. Martin's Press

Printed in Mexico
1 2 3 4 5 6 7 22 21 20 19 18

For Edgar,
who started it all

THOSE WHO'VE CLUED POE

I would like to thank my merry band of mischief makers, without whom this book would not have been possible. I'd be willing to wager each and every one of them has used Poe in a crossword at one time or another.

Will Shortz, *New York Times* crossword puzzle editor, constructed the Sudoku used in this book. Even though it is all numbers, I would not be surprised to find the word Poe hidden there somewhere.

Fred Piscop constructed the crosswords, almost before I asked for them. Soon he'll be constructing them before I even write the book.

Ellen Ripstein, the American Crossword Tournament champion, edited the puzzles and saved me, once again, from my mistakes.

The Puzzle Lady thanks them.

CHAPTER 1

"I have a puzzle for you."

Cora Felton winced. She regarded the eager girl looking up at her much in the way a person might regard a particularly irritating gnat. She took a breath and forced a rather frosty smile. "No, you don't."

"Yes, I do. I have a crossword puzzle for you."

"You may have a crossword puzzle, but it's not for me. It's for you. And you should work at it until you solve it."

"But you're the Puzzle Lady."

Cora Felton grimaced. She *was* the Puzzle Lady, much to her chagrin. She had a nationally syndicated crossword puzzle column and a series of TV ads hawking a breakfast cereal to schoolchildren. In both cases she was a total fraud. She didn't eat the cereal and she couldn't do the puzzles. Her niece Sherry was the brains of the outfit. Sherry created the puzzles and wrote

9

the column and sent it off to syndication. All that Cora contributed was the smiling, grandmotherly face that graced the column.

Because of this, Cora was constantly being ambushed by people who wanted her to talk about crossword puzzles or, worse, solve crossword puzzles, which she had about as much chance of doing as she had of swimming the English Channel.

Today she had just stopped into Cushman's Bake Shop for a cranberry scone, of which she was particularly fond. Mrs. Cushman couldn't bake a lick and trucked in all her pastries from the Silver Moon Bakery in Manhattan, so her wares were top-notch and demand was high. Cora was waiting at the counter, and the last thing she needed was to be distracted by a fan and lose her place in line.

Over the years Cora had become quite adept at sidestepping annoying people who wanted to pester her about puzzles. But this was a young girl. Of that she was quite certain. Cora had reached the age where girls she thought were teenagers often turned out to be twenty-eight or even thirty-five, but she would have made book on the fact the bright-eyed, fresh-faced young thing in the ponytail and retainer was under twenty. This was definitely a schoolgirl, and disappointing children was a serious matter. There was even a clause in her contract with Granville Grains Cereal that triggered a termination-without-compensation option in that instance.

"And who might you be, young lady?"

"Peggy Dawson." From the girl's somewhat pained inflection, Cora had probably met her before, though she had no recollection of it.

"Well, listen, Peggy Dawson. I'll tell you what I'll do. Give me your puzzle and I'll take it home, and when I get some time I'll look at it. I'm not promising anything, you understand. I get so many crosswords. I can't solve them all."

Cora had been particularly pleased when she came up with that excuse. It was absolutely true. She couldn't solve them all. In point of fact, she couldn't solve a single one, but that minor detail got lost in the shuffle.

Peggy Dawson's face left no doubt as to her youth. "But I *need* it solved," she said. She looked like she might stamp her foot. "Or I won't know what it says."

"That is absolutely true," Cora said. "If you don't solve it, you won't know what it says."

Cora had reached the front of the line. Mrs. Cushman smiled at her. "And what

11

will it be today?"

"A cranberry scone. Please tell me you're not out of them."

"You're just in time. I've got two left."

Cora was tempted to buy both of them and save one for later, but that wouldn't help her fit into her new dress, which she had bought a trifle on the small side as an incentive to lose weight. Her closet was full of clothes she had bought on that basis.

"I'll have a latte and a scone," Cora said.

"One latte," Mrs. Cushman called to her helper. She rang Cora up, gave her the scone, and made change.

Cora moved down the counter and picked up her latte. She took a greedy bite of the scone and turned away from the counter to find the girl still standing there. Somehow Cora had expected her to be gone.

"That won't do at all." Peggy picked up the conversation as if there had been no interruption. "I'm really worried about this puzzle, and I've got to know what it means. Won't you help me? It's a mystery. I thought you liked mysteries."

"How is it a mystery?"

"I don't know who sent it, and I don't know why. Look, my truck's right outside. Let's take a run out to my house and I can give you the puzzle and we can clean all this up."

Cora was astonished at how the girl had steamrolled over all her objections by simply ignoring them. It seemed like the only way to get rid of the girl would be to take out a gun and shoot her. It occurred to her Granville Grains probably had a clause in her contract about *that*.

Harvey Beerbaum banged in the door. He waved at Cora and took his place in line. Her answering wave was less enthusiastic. The pudgy gentleman in the tweedy suit and tie was a terrible bore, constantly pestering her with his attentions. Cora was never sure whether he was hitting on her or if he was actually gay.

Worse, the man was a genuine cruciverbalist, who constructed puzzles for *The New York Times* and could never understand why she was not just dying to talk about them.

If the truth be known, Harvey Beerbaum was even more annoying than the maddening girl.

Cora's eyes widened.

She glanced from one to the other and practically purred.

Cora put on her most coy and coquettish face, batted her eyes, and managed a singsong lilt to her voice.

"Har-vey."

13

CHAPTER 2

"Are you sure you're old enough to drive?" Harvey Beerbaum said. Harvey hadn't been happy when Cora sent him along in her place. He was even less so when he found out it meant Peggy would be driving.

Harvey was jouncing along on the passenger seat of Peggy's pickup truck. The dirt road up which she lived had a number of ruts and potholes, which the girl seemed to be ignoring and driving right through.

"I'm sixteen," Peggy said.

That did not cheer him. While she was indeed old enough to drive, it occurred to Harvey that at least they weren't crossing any state lines. He found the fact he'd even had that thought unsettling.

Without any warning, Peggy swerved to the left up a dirt road even bumpier than the one they had just left. It wound around and stopped by an old farmhouse on the side of the hill. A rocky overgrown meadow stretched out in front of it. Had a farmer ever plowed the field, he would have experienced a tractor ride even worse than the journey Harvey had just enjoyed in the truck.

"Here we are," Peggy announced cheerfully. She had the door open and was out of the truck before he had even righted himself.

Harvey slid down from the passenger seat. The ground seemed farther than he'd anticipated. He caught his balance, straightened his jacket and tie.

"Come on, let's get the puzzle," Peggy said, hopping up on the porch.

"Why don't you bring it out?"

"Oh, don't be an old stick-in-the-mud."

"Is anyone at home?"

"Johnny's here. That's his car."

"Johnny?"

"My brother."

As if on cue, a young man came out the front door. At least young by Harvey's standards. He was certainly older than the girl. Late twenties, perhaps. Rugged type. He wore a jacket and tie, and looked somewhat uncomfortable in it, as if he'd be more natural in sweatpants and a T-shirt. He took one look at Harvey and demanded, "Who's he?"

Harvey was somewhat taken aback, but he forced a smile. "I'm Harvey Beerbaum."

The young man scowled at his sister. "Come on, Peggy, we talked about this. You can't bring men around when I'm not here."

"You're here."

"I'm going out."

"And that's my fault?"

"He can't be here. No offense," Johnny said. "My sister's young, she doesn't know what's appropriate."

"I'm not young."

"See?" Johnny smiled, which softened the rudeness. Harvey figured he could probably get away with a lot with that smile.

"She just wanted help with the crossword puzzle," Harvey said.

"The what?"

"I'm good with crossword puzzles."

"You can't go in the house. She doesn't understand, but I'm sure you do."

"I'm not going in the house. We just came to get the puzzle."

"Where's the puzzle?"

"In my *room,*" Peggy said impatiently. "Where did you think it was?"

"Well, he's not going up there. You get the puzzle and bring it down."

"Fine," Peggy said. Her attitude indicated it wasn't fine, but her brother was a moron

16

and there was no use arguing.

"I gotta go," Johnny said. He pointed at Harvey. "I'm counting on you to do the right thing."

Harvey nearly said, "Yes, sir."

Johnny got in his car and drove away.

Peggy clapped her hands together. "Great. Come on."

"What?" Harvey said.

"Let's go get the puzzle."

"Your brother doesn't want me in the house."

"He's gone."

"I'm not going in the house."

"Oh, come on."

"You heard what your brother said. Get the puzzle and bring it down."

"Fine."

Peggy stomped off into the house.

She was back in minutes. "It's gone!"

"What?"

"The puzzle. Someone took it."

"Oh, for goodness' sakes. Why would anyone take a puzzle?"

"I don't know, but someone did. It was right on my desk. Now it's not."

"Are you sure?"

"Sure I'm sure. It was right there in plain sight."

"Who else is here?"

17

"No one. No one's here."

"Isn't it possible you put it away and forgot you moved it?"

"No, it's not possible. If I moved it, I'd know I moved it. And I didn't move it. It was right on the desk and it's gone. I'll show you."

"Show me what?"

"The desk. Where it was taken."

"If it's gone, there's nothing to see. And your brother doesn't want me in the house."

"That was before someone stole my puzzle. You think he wants people coming in stealing things? That's why he doesn't want me bringing people by."

Harvey thought that wasn't even remotely why Peggy's brother didn't want her bringing people by, but he wasn't about to argue.

He wasn't about to go in the house, either.

"My dear young lady. This is not what I signed on for. It is frankly out of my field of expertise. Cora Felton asked me to help you with a puzzle. The fact that the puzzle is missing throws the ball back in her court."

"But she doesn't want the ball," Peggy complained, in the peevish voice seemingly trademarked by disappointed teenagers.

"Failing that, young lady, there is an excellent course open to you."

Peggy scrunched up her nose. "Do you

enjoy confusing people?"

"I'm sorry. That was not my intention. If you really believe the puzzle has been stolen, there is only one thing to do."

"What's that?"

"Go to the police."

CHAPTER 3

Cora came out the front door of Cushman's Bake Shop and nearly dropped her latte. She stood on the sidewalk, blinking. Surely it was the bright morning sun that was distorting her vision, making her think she had seen things that she hadn't. The man getting out of the car across Main Street in front of the library couldn't be whom she thought.

His hair was way too dark for a man his age, screamed of dye, or hair plugs, or even a wig. And his suit was shiny. The sun reflected off it in a blinding glare.

He turned, and the light fell on his face.

"Melvin!" Cora gasped.

Cora's least favorite ex-husband saw her and smiled, the same ingratiating grin that had caused women who should have known better to lose their minds, to think this subhuman specimen of masculinity was not only acceptable but damn near irresistible.

Cora had married him once. Granted it was back in the days when she was drinking, but that was no excuse. The man held a strange fascination.

"Hi, Cora," Melvin called. He crossed his legs, leaned back against the side of his car, making her come to him, just like in the old days. She was tempted to walk away and leave him hanging.

Instead, she took a bite of scone, washed it down with sip of coffee, and stepped off the curb.

A car nearly ran her down. The driver hit the horn. Cora saw to her embarrassment it was First Selectman Iris Cooper. That was sure to be the talk of the next bridge game.

Cora looked both ways, continued to cross the street.

"Melvin, what are you doing here?"

Melvin grinned. "I don't see why you're so surprised. It's not like you haven't seen me lately."

"I've seen you in New York. I haven't seen you in Bakerhaven."

"It's awhile since I've been back. But you know, I miss this place."

"No, I don't know that, Melvin. Tell me how you miss this place enough to come driving up."

"Could I have some of that scone?"

Cora jerked her thumb over her shoulder. "Cushman's Bake Shop. If you hurry, they have one left."

"Just helping you maintain your trim figure."

"That's not going to get you anywhere, Melvin."

"Is it going to get me a scone?"

Cora broke off a piece, handed it to him. "Here, if it will shut you up. What are you doing here?"

"Would you believe I came to see you?"

"No."

"Well, that's honest enough. All right, I'm scouting some real estate."

"No, Melvin, you're not."

"Why not?"

"Because that's a legitimate enterprise. If you're involved in something, it must be nefarious."

"Oh, big word. You must do crosswords, or something."

Cora flinched. Melvin was one of the people who knew she was a fraud. He was also unscrupulous enough to reveal it.

"I know you, Melvin. You're changing the subject like you had something to hide."

Melvin grinned. "She said, changing the subject."

"You're the subject, Melvin. I have a right

to be in Bakerhaven. You, on the other hand, can't justify your existence."

"You mean my presence. That's pretty sloppy for a wordsmith."

"I mean existence. You can't justify your presence either, but that's a lesser issue. You wanna walk me through the real estate bit?"

"I thought you didn't believe the real estate bit."

"I don't, but I'll humor you."

"I'm scamming the real estate market."

"Why?"

"Ah. Manhattan prices are through the roof. People are leaving town. The suburbs are filling up, so people are moving farther out and commuting longer distances. Bakerhaven is the new Scarsdale."

"Tell me you didn't say that."

"Anyway, the real estate market's a gold mine."

"But you're not a real estate broker."

"No, but Judy Douglas Knauer is. I can lay ten percent on top of her price and the sucker thinks he's getting a deal."

"That sounds more like you, Melvin."

"Thank you. I hope you didn't think I'd gone legit."

"You're really up here flimflamming the real estate market?"

"That, or I came to see you."

"Where's your girlfriend?"

"What girlfriend?"

"You're never without a girlfriend. Where have you got her stashed?"

Melvin grinned, showed his cuffs like a magician. "Nothing up my sleeve. I'm in between girlfriends at the moment."

"Hold the phone," Cora said. "You're up here pulling a semilegitimate real estate scam instead of dealing three-card monte, and you're traveling alone? What the hell is going on here?"

"See, maybe I came to see you. You have a boyfriend at the moment?"

"That's none of your business."

"Actually, it is. If you remarry, it's the end of my alimony payments."

"If I remarry, hell will have frozen over."

"You say that now, but let an eligible bachelor come around."

"Eligible bachelor?"

"You prefer the term 'wealthy widower'? So, assume I came to see you. You're looking awfully good. I'm staying at that motel out past the mall. You wanna drop by for a matinee?"

"In your dreams, Melvin."

Melvin whipped out his iPhone. "I'll call you. What's your cell phone number?"

"I don't have a cell phone."

"You're kidding. How do you take self-ies?"

"Why in the world would I do that?"

"Come on, Cora. Get with the times. How you gonna sell cereal to kids if you can't relate? Here." Melvin threw his arm around her shoulders. He leaned his head next to hers and held out his phone. "Smile!"

The look Cora gave him could have stopped a charging rhino.

Melvin smiled, snapped the selfie. He checked the picture. "Perfect."

CHAPTER 4

Chief Dale Harper regarded the girl dubiously. As a small-town police chief, he was used to dealing with all sorts of situations, but this was somewhat out of his line.

"Someone stole your puzzle?"

"Yes."

"Why would they do that?"

"I have no idea."

"Well, that's what I need to know. Who had the motive, the means, and the opportunity. That's how we go about solving crimes."

Peggy made a face. "Please. I am not a child. I don't need a lecture on criminology."

Chief Harper had to disagree. The girl was younger than his daughter Clara. Never mind that Clara was long out of college, anyone younger than his daughter was a child, and always would be. "Can you think of any reason why anyone would take your crossword puzzle?"

"No."

"What was it about?"

"What?"

"The crossword puzzle. What did it have to do with?"

"I don't know."

"You didn't solve it?"

"I don't know anything about crossword puzzles."

"Where did you get it?"

"It was slipped under my door."

"The door of your house?"

"The door of my room. If it was under the door of my house, I wouldn't know it was for me."

"It wasn't in an envelope?"

"No. It was folded like it was in an envelope and slipped under my door."

"Where is your house?"

"Out on Colson Road. The old farmhouse. We moved in last year."

"Who else lives there?"

"Just me and my brother."

Chief Harper remembered vaguely. If it was who he was thinking of, the parents had been killed in a car accident, and the brother had come home from the war to take charge. "Your brother's a soldier?"

"Was. They sent him home. Stupid, if you

ask me. I can take care of myself."

Harper wasn't so sure about that. The girl seemed younger every time she opened her mouth. "Did you ask him about the crossword puzzle?"

"Why would I do that?"

"Maybe he slipped it under your door."

"Why would he do that? He doesn't do crosswords, and he knows I don't."

"Okay," Chief Harper said. "Let me get this straight. Someone stole your crossword puzzle. You don't know who took it, you don't know where it came from, and you don't know what it says."

"You sound like I'm making it up."

"Not at all. But did you know there's a person in town who specializes in crossword puzzles?"

"Yeah. Cora Felton. I asked her to solve it, but she wouldn't do it. Gave me this other guy she said was a real hotshot. Only when it turned up missing, he didn't want anything to do with it."

"What did he say?"

"He told me to come to you." Peggy looked at him with accusing eyes. "He said you'd help me."

Chief Harper sighed. He wasn't sure whom he blamed more, Harvey or Cora.

Yes, he was.

28

As soon as the girl was gone, he reached for the phone.

CHAPTER 5

"Can I sleep with Melvin?"

Becky Baldwin dropped her pen. The young, blond attorney who would have looked right at home in a *Sports Illustrated* swimsuit edition was actually a veteran courtroom strategist, practiced in maintaining a poker face.

Not today. She gawked up at Cora. "What?"

"My ex-husband's in town. With no bimbo in tow. It's a rare opportunity. I could take advantage of it."

"You want my permission?"

"I'd like your legal opinion."

"My legal opinion is you're out of your mind."

"That's a little hasty, don't you think? You didn't even look up a precedent."

"I don't have to look up precedents when it's Melvin. I know Melvin. He's bad news. Anything involving Melvin is a bad idea."

30

"That's unkind."

"Unkind? It's high praise compared to some of the things you've said about Melvin."

"Yeah, sure, but I've been married to him. That's your whole problem. You've never been married. You can't really appreciate these situations until you've been ground into the dirt."

"That's your assessment of marriage?"

"That's my assessment of Melvin. The man's a walking disaster."

"And you'd like to sleep with him."

" 'Like' is a strong word."

Becky put up her hand. "No, you're not going to spoil my day."

"You're having a good day?"

"That I am."

"What are you doing?"

"I'm doing my taxes."

"That's a good day?"

"It is this year. Usually I'm looking at negative net gain, trying to see if my expenses justify my paying nothing. This year I actually made money."

"Then I clearly haven't been charging you enough for my services," Cora said. Cora occasionally did freelance detective work for Becky. On more than one of those occasions, Cora herself had been the defendant.

31

"Good. Then I don't feel so bad coming to you for free advice."

"Are you serious?"

"Of course, I'm serious. You think I want your permission to sleep with Melvin? I want to know if sleeping with someone could be construed as reconciliation and grounds for termination of alimony payments."

"Only if he's an unscrupulous bastard."

"That goes without saying." Cora took a breath. "Okay, if Melvin were to raise the issue, would you be able to fight it?"

"You want to know whether, if you sleep with Melvin, giving him grounds to terminate your alimony, I would be able to beat it in court?"

"Would you?"

"I don't believe you're even asking the question."

"That doesn't get you out of answering it."

"Get me out of? You're asking me for free advice and acting like I have an obligation."

"I'd pay you if we went to court."

"That's nice of you. Why is Melvin here?"

"He's working a real estate scam, selling houses he doesn't own."

"Somehow that sounds illegal."

"It probably is. He makes it sound legit."

"I'm sure he does. Well, I see some more work on the horizon, defending you from an aiding and abetting charge."

"I am not aiding and abetting Melvin."

"Of course not. When the police break down the door and catch you in bed with him, I'm sure they'll assume you're working independently."

The phone rang.

Becky scooped it up. "Becky Baldwin . . . Uh huh . . . She's right here . . . Okay, I'll tell her."

Becky hung up the phone, cocked her head at Cora. "Are you sure Melvin hasn't conned you into anything illegal yet?"

"I'm sure. Why?"

"The police want to see you."

CHAPTER 6

"I have a crime and it's right up your alley."

Cora regarded the chief suspiciously. "What alley is that?"

"Don't be like that, Cora. You know I always come to you when the police are stumped."

"You're stumped?"

"Absolutely."

"And you don't know where to turn?"

"Not at all."

"Is there a puzzle involved?"

"Yes and no."

"You lost me, Chief. You had me at crime and you lost me at yes and no. Particularly pertaining to a puzzle."

Harper rubbed his chin. "I'm telling this all wrong. It's a robbery."

"What was stolen?"

"Well, that's the thing."

"You tell me it's a puzzle and I'll scream."

"It's a puzzle."

"Did you just say that to see if I would?"

"No. Apparently, you sent Harvey Beerbaum out to some girl's house to solve her crossword puzzle, and the puzzle's gone."

"You mean she couldn't find it?"

"Yes."

"Isn't it more likely mislaid than stolen?"

"That's what I'd like you to tell me."

"I just did."

"I don't need a premise, I need an answer."

"Did you know Melvin's in town?"

"You think he took the puzzle?"

"No. I was trying to change the subject."

"Boy, I wish I could do that. A crime happens, I can't deal with it. So what do I do? I simply change the subject."

"Melvin is a subject changer."

"I understand. Your ex-husband reduces you to a mindless adolescent. What you need is mental stimulation. Particularly when it's a problem of your own making."

"*My* making?"

"You sent Harvey Beerbaum to solve the puzzle. The puzzle is not there. Harvey is not capable of dealing with its disappearance and bails out. Left in the lurch, the girl turns to me. She's reported a robbery, and I have to deal with it."

"Yes, you do."

"And I am. By reporting it to the proper authorities."

"I'm the proper authority?"

"Best I can think of. A puzzle that mysteriously disappeared. What could be better?"

"A puzzle that has nothing to do with me."

"This has something to do with you. As I have outlined."

"I'd like to help you out, Chief. But I happen to have my hands full. Did I mention that Melvin's in town?"

"I do not want to hear the name Melvin again."

Dan Finley came in the door. "Hi, Cora. You know Melvin's in town?"

"Really?" Cora shot a look at the chief. "That's a shock. Tell me all about it."

"She knows her ex-husband's in town," Harper said. "She's been driving me crazy about it, trying to get out of solving my robbery."

"You got a robbery, Chief?"

"See?" Cora said. "There's the man you should be putting on this. He's much closer to the victim's age. They might wind up getting married."

"Not unless he wants to go to jail," Harper said. "But that's an excellent idea. Dan, the victim's name is Peggy Dawson. She lives out on Colson Road. Run out there, case the scene, see what you can find. I want a thorough investigation. Leave no stone unturned."

"Absolutely, Chief. What's the case?"

"It's a sensitive case requiring tact and diplomacy."

"You see why the chief doesn't want to take it," Cora said.

"The victim is a teenage girl. She could be making the whole thing up, but I don't think so. She doesn't seem delusional, and she's not that kind of mean."

"Gotcha," Dan said. "So you want me to take her story at face value while viewing it with the appropriate amount of skepticism."

"That's not even remotely what I said, but never mind. I want you to investigate this, largely so she can see we are. I don't expect you to have much success."

"Why not?"

Harper put up his hand. "No offense meant. It's just that short of finding the missing property, I don't expect you to be able to do much."

"Why?"

"I'm not impugning your ability, I —"

"Oh, for God's sakes, Chief," Cora said impatiently, "stop drawing it out. The girl thinks someone stole her crossword puzzle."

Dan looked at the chief. "Her crossword

puzzle?"

"That's right."

"That doesn't make any sense."

"Welcome to the club," Cora said.

"It does seem unlikely," Harper said. "But she's rather certain. So try not to act like you've been assigned something stupid."

"Yeah, sure, Chief, But —"

"But what?"

"Well, you know I'm a big fan of the Puzzle Lady, always have been. But as a celebrity. I don't actually know anything about crosswords."

"Do you know what they look like?"

"Yes, of course."

"Then you can look for one."

"Okay."

Cora beamed, delighted at how adroitly she had gotten out of that one, shifting the burden to Dan Finley.

"Of course I could sure use help with the puzzle."

"Take Cora."

Chapter 7

"This is fun," Dan Finley said as he drove
out to Peggy Dawson's house.

"I'm glad you think so," Cora grumbled.
"As far as I'm concerned, it's just another
crossword puzzle."

"It's a *stolen* crossword puzzle," Dan said.
"That's interesting. Has that ever happened
before?"

"Not often enough. I wish someone would
steal all the crossword puzzles Chief Harper
tried to involve me in."

"Think of it as a robbery. Pretend it's not
a puzzle. Pretend it's a valuable diamond
necklace and the chief won't let you go."

"Why wouldn't he let me go? He's taken
me along on a liquor store robbery and an
antiques shop break-in. Why not a diamond
necklace?"

"Well, it's worth a lot of money."

"Oh, you mean I'm good enough for petty
theft but not capital crimes?"

39

"He's brought you in on murders."

"Yes, when it involved a puzzle."

Dan glanced over at her. "What are you all cranky for? Is it because Melvin's in town."

"Why would that make me cranky?"

"Melvin always makes you cranky. You can't say his name without getting a homicidal look in your eye."

"Nonsense. I've gotten over Melvin."

Dan Finley was suddenly very busy watching the road. He was relieved when they bounced to a stop in front of the farmhouse.

Peggy Dawson was waiting outside. "Well, that's more like it. I thought the police weren't going to take me seriously. And you," she said to Cora, "pawning me off on Harvey what's-his-name. He wouldn't even come in the house."

Cora suppressed a smile. "Was anyone at home?"

"My brother. Well, he had to leave, but he was here when we got here."

"And you went in and found the puzzle missing?"

"Yes. And Harvey big-shot puzzle maker wouldn't even look. He just told me to go to the police. So I went to the police, and they didn't do anything."

"I'm right here." Dan Finley smiled at her.

40

"Let's see if we can figure out how this puzzle was taken."

"How are you going to do that?"

"We'll start by inspecting the scene of the crime. Where was the puzzle?"

"In my room. Upstairs."

"You see why Harvey wasn't thrilled?" Cora said.

"Let's take a look," Dan said.

Peggy led Dan through the foyer and up the front stairs. Cora tagged along behind.

"Oh, *now* you're interested?" Peggy said.

"Dan's an old friend."

"What does that mean?"

"It means a lot," Cora said. "Show us the puzzle."

"I can't show you the puzzle. Someone took it."

"Can you show us where it was?"

Peggy rolled her eyes. "Of course I can."

Dan shot Cora a warning look. He wasn't really afraid of an all-out catfight between a teenage girl and the world-famous Puzzle Lady, but he wasn't ruling it out. "You say the puzzle was slipped under your door?"

"Yes."

"Were you home at the time?"

"No. I came back and found it."

"Was your door open or closed?"

"If it was open, it couldn't be slipped

41

under it."

Cora shot Dan a look, delighted he wasn't having an easy time of it, either.

The second floor was your typical New England farmhouse, a narrow hallway with bedrooms and a central bathroom. With a teenage girl it was probably hell in the mornings.

"Which room is yours?" Dan said.

"Right here."

"Your door's open now," Cora said.

"Yeah. Because I'm home. When I'm out I close my door."

"And lock it?"

"Why would I lock it?"

Cora stifled the urge to say, Why do you close it if you don't lock it? Dan Finley's elbow in her ribs might have had something to do with that.

Peggy swept into the room, which revealed a girl on the cusp of womanhood. Dolls and stuffed animals mingled with posters of pop stars. Cora couldn't name a single one. She wasn't sure if that should make her feel superior or just old.

The furniture was wooden, had most likely come with the house. The single bed on a metal frame resembled an army cot. It was offset with comforters. A thin layer of scattered garments complimented the throw rug on the wooden floor.

A laptop computer sat open on a wooden desk. Peggy pushed ahead and closed it.

"So where was the puzzle?" Dan Finley said.

"Right here." Peggy pointed to the desk next to the laptop.

"On the desk?"

"Yes."

"Next to the laptop?"

"That's right."

"The laptop was there when the puzzle was taken?"

"Yes."

"Someone took the puzzle and left the laptop?"

Peggy's look said *Duh.* "The laptop's still here."

"I see that. You wanna lift it up?"

"The puzzle's not under the laptop."

"Lift it up."

Peggy lifted the laptop. "See?"

"Turn the laptop over."

"Why?"

"It might be stuck to the bottom."

"It isn't."

"Turn it over."

Peggy turned the laptop over. "Told you."

"Well, it's not there now."

"It was never there."

"Did you look?"

"What?"

"When you found the puzzle was missing? Did you look under the laptop?"

"No."

"Why not?"

"Because it wasn't there. Please. You're asking silly questions. Can't you find my puzzle?"

"I'm beginning to strongly doubt it," Cora said. "Did you ask your brother if he took the puzzle?"

"He wasn't here."

"So you're the only one who saw it?"

Peggy's eyes widened. "Now you don't believe me?"

"We believe you," Dan Finley said soothingly. "We just want to eliminate all the places a puzzle might be."

"Might be?" Peggy said. "It was right there."

"Well, it's not there now," Cora said.

"Yeah, but what if it is?" Dan was getting a kick out of the idea. "Isn't there a short story like that? The stolen letter is hidden in plain sight where no one can find it. Maybe that's what happened here."

"That's 'The Purloined Letter' by Edgar Allan Poe. And there's no parallel at all. The letter was hidden in the apartment of

44

the man who stole it. The police knew it was there, they just couldn't find it. We're in the room of the person it was stolen *from.* If it was here, it wouldn't be stolen at all."

"Even so."

"Even so, Dan? That's like saying a kumquat isn't quite the same as a snowblower."

Peggy was looking back and forth like a spectator at a tennis match. She'd been trying to follow the conversation, but kumquats and snowblowers was too much. "What are you two *talking* about? My puzzle was stolen. It's a simple crime. The type you handle every day. Why is this so hard?"

"You wanna take that one, Cora?" Dan said.

"Not really, but I'll give it a try. The problem here is, the value of the article taken raises doubts as to the probability of actual theft, suggesting it was merely mislaid."

Peggy stuck her chin out defiantly. "That would be true if we knew the value of the article taken. But we don't know the value of the article taken because the puzzle wasn't solved. If it had been solved, it might be very valuable to some person for some reason or other. I don't know who and I don't know why. That's not my department. That's supposedly yours. But if you ask me, there's every indication that puzzle is extremely valuable."

"Oh," Dan said. "And why is that?"

Peggy looked at him as if he were a moron. "Because it's gone."

CHAPTER 8

Peggy, Dan, and Cora came out the front door of the farmhouse to find Peggy's brother on his way in from the car.

"So you sent for reinforcements?" he said. "What, that other guy couldn't handle it?"

"The puzzle was stolen."

"What?"

"Someone came in my room and took it. Was it you?"

"Why would I do that?"

Cora smiled. The man was way too young for her, still it was a reflex reaction to a handsome man. "If we knew your motive, we'd be hauling you downtown," she said good-naturedly. "Your sister reported her puzzle stolen. She'd like us to find it. You didn't take it, did you? Just to look at, perhaps?"

"Of course not. Why would I care about a crossword puzzle," he said. Then, realizing she was the Puzzle Lady, added, "No offense meant."

"Oh, none taken. I quite agree. It's just a stupid puzzle. But if it's stolen property, it needs to be recovered."

"Well, good luck with that."

"Thank you," Dan Finley said. "And you could help us. Is your room upstairs?"

"Yeah."

"You mind letting us look around? If the puzzle got moved from one room to another for any reason, it would be nice to put this case to bed."

"There's no point. It isn't in my room."

Cora smiled. "I'm afraid that wouldn't satisfy a police report. Self-serving declaration, you understand."

"I understand, I just can't help you. The puzzle isn't there."

"So you wouldn't mind letting us see?"

He frowned. "I would, actually. I told you it isn't there, and I don't lie. I mean, come on, Peggy, would I take your puzzle? I didn't even know you had one."

"Maybe not," Cora said. "But if you were walking by her door and just saw it on her desk . . ."

"Walking by her door? She's at the end of the hall. I don't walk by her door."

"Or if she forgot she was holding the puzzle and accidentally left it in your room."

"Peggy doesn't go in my room. And I don't go in hers. We respect each other's property."

"Then you must be up for Siblings of the Month," Cora said. "Brothers and sisters usually fight like cats and dogs. Anyway, it's foolish to try to come up with scenarios in which this could have happened. The question is whether it could have happened at all. And it's easily answered by taking a look at your room."

"I'll look at my room. And if I find the puzzle, I'll let you know. Or I'll just give it to her, which would be more convenient since she happens to live here."

Dan Finley's interest was perking up. "You're not going to let us look in your room?"

"Not unless you have a search warrant."

"That's rather silly, under the circumstances."

"Oh, for goodness' sakes, Johnny," Peggy said. "Let them look in your room and be done with it. I want them to find my puzzle. They're never going to do it while they're hung up on you."

"Sorry. It's a matter of principle. I'm willing to fight for my country, but I'm not willing to give up the freedoms I'm fighting for."

"I understand," Dan Finley said. "Okay,

Cora, let's go."

"You're giving up just like that?" Peggy said incredulously.

"Not at all. But your brother's right. We can't search his room without a warrant."

Dan and Cora climbed into the police car. "Are you getting a warrant?" Peggy said.

Dan stuck his head out the window. "That's up to the chief."

CHAPTER 9

"Well, that's interesting," Dan said as they drove away.

"Not really," Cora said.

"Are you kidding me? The brother, a total nonstarter, is suddenly a person of interest in the crime. Demanding a search warrant. How stupid is that?"

"I'd say it's high on the list."

"It's practically a confession. No, I didn't take the puzzle, and if you don't believe me that's tough, but I won't let you look and see."

"You think he stole the puzzle?"

"Isn't it obvious?"

"Not to me."

"Oh, come on, Cora. Are you kidding me? What, a handsome man, he must be innocent?"

"That hadn't even occurred to me."

"Maybe not consciously. I'm just saying. Those are the actions of a guilty man. Why

51

would you think anything else?"

"I've been married to some guilty men. At least guilty of something. Usually it wasn't felonies. Unless you count Melvin."

"Come on, Cora. If the guy didn't take the puzzle, why wouldn't he want to prove it?"

"I don't know. Maybe he's got drugs. Or a bunch of porn mags."

"Why do you say that?"

"Oh, you come on. The guy doesn't want us to search his room. What's he more likely not to want us to find? Drugs, pornography, or a crossword puzzle?"

"Yeah, but if he *stole* the crossword puzzle . . ."

"Then the whole world is turned upside down. Crossword puzzle theft is not high on your list of felonies. Unless you count plagiarism, and I try not to count plagiarism because it gives me a headache. I like a crime you can actually see. Anyway, demanding a search warrant isn't the act of a man with a crossword puzzle. It's the act of a man with a murder weapon."

"Too bad no one's been murdered," Dan said.

"Bite your tongue."

"Well, for my money the guy has the crossword puzzle, and as soon as we were out of there he put the puzzle someplace where his sister would find it, so she'd call up and tell us we can stop looking for it."

"That's not going to happen. But if it does, you don't say, 'Fine, we'll swing by and pick it up.' You say, 'Fine, now you can give it to Harvey Beerbaum and get it solved.' Just keep me out of it. I've already had more trouble than I can stand over a puzzle that may not even exist."

The police radio crackled.

Dan scooped it up. "Yeah, Chief."

"You on your way back from the girl's house?"

"That's right."

"Better turn around. Her brother just called."

Dan shot Cora a look of triumph. "Cora doesn't want to, Chief. She says give the puzzle to Harvey."

"What puzzle?"

"Didn't her brother find a crossword puzzle?"

"No. He found a bloodstained knife."

CHAPTER 10

Dan Finley pointed to the knife on Johnny's desk. "This is where you found it?"

"No, it was under my pillow."

"You picked it up?"

"Well, I wasn't going to leave it there."

"Why'd you look under your pillow?"

"Because of what you said. You made such a fuss about someone could have left it in my room. So I went up to my room to look."

"You searched your room?"

"No, I just looked around."

"Why'd you look under your pillow?"

"The bed was made. The pillow should have been straight, but it was actually askew. I didn't leave it that way. So I looked."

"That's not your knife?" Cora said.

"Of course not. If it was my knife, I'd have cleaned it and put it away."

"You're used to cleaning bloody knives?"

"Lady, I was in combat. I seen a lot worse than a bloody knife. My own equipment I keep clean. Because it could save your life."

Dan Finley took out a plastic evidence bag. "All right, I'll bag this, for all the good it'll do. I'm going to need your fingerprints for comparison. I hope there's some on the knife that aren't yours."

"Anyone been stabbed with a knife recently?" Cora said.

Peggy gave her a look.

Cora shrugged. "Well, you can't have somebody stabbed with a knife without a somebody. Not that I'm wishing anyone harm, but if they've already had it, it would be nice to know."

"Is she always this weird?" Peggy asked Dan.

"No, she's on her best behavior," Dan said. "Usually she's positively loopy."

"We're not trying to give you a hard time," Cora said. "But you start out with a stolen puzzle and you find a bloody knife, and there's no rhyme or reason for either occurrence, I would have to argue it's not me that's odd."

"You're saying it's odd I reported the knife?" Johnny said. "If it turned out something was wrong and I didn't report the knife, you'd be making a big deal out of the fact I didn't."

"You absolutely did the right thing," Dan

Finley said. "No question. Now then, do you know anyone who has a knife like this? Is there anyone around who could have left this knife?"

"I've been working, so I haven't been around much."

"Oh? What do you do?"

"I show houses for Judy Douglas Knauer."

CHAPTER 11

"What's the matter, Cora?" Chief Harper said.

Dan Finley had dropped Cora off at the police station. She'd been on her way to her car when the chief ran out to stop her.

"What do you mean, what's the matter? Nothing's the matter."

"Dan Finley said this guy mentioned working for Judy Douglas Knauer and you went white as a sheet."

"Dan's young and impressionable."

"Dan's not that young and not that impressionable. He knows you all too well. The guy with the bloody knife works for Judy Douglas Knauer. Why does that frighten you?"

"Melvin's working with Judy Douglas Knauer."

"I see. So you immediately envision the bloodstained corpse of Judy Douglas Knauer popping up and Melvin in jail for the murder."

"That's ridiculous."

"I'm not claiming it happened. I'm saying that was your first thought."

"Melvin's not a killer."

"He's never been caught."

"He's never been caught because he doesn't do the crime. Good God, you're making all this up from Dan Finley's impression of my reaction?"

"I'm making all this up from the fact I have an unaccounted for bloody knife. It's somewhat unusual to have a murder weapon without a crime. Nonetheless, I'm treating it seriously. I'm having the fingerprints lifted, and I'm having the blood analyzed. So if a dead body does drop in my lap, I won't be caught flatfooted. Now, since you have your own irrational suspicions, if you want to help me out, why don't you call Judy Douglas Knauer and ask her if she's still alive. And if you've got his cell phone number, I suggest you call Melvin, too."

"I don't have Melvin's cell phone number."

"Get it from Judy."

CHAPTER 12

"Do you know Johnny Dawson?"

Melvin greeted the question with a short, pungent expletive.

"I take it you do," Cora said.

Cora had tracked Melvin down at the bar in the Country Kitchen by the simple expedient of calling his cell phone. She had his cell phone number, though she felt no inclination to let Chief Harper in on the fact. But Melvin, no matter how unlikable, undesirable, or in or out of favor, was a man of many talents, who often was useful in a delicate situation, such as when someone needed to be blackmailed, extorted, or bluffed.

"He's too young for you, Cora. Hell, he's too young for your *daughter.*"

"I don't have a daughter."

"I rest my case. Good-looking mindless boys that age are a menace. They shouldn't be allowed."

"What's he done to you?

"He hasn't done anything to me. He hasn't noticed me. I don't think he knows I exist. Come on. I mean, here I am, all set to run a perfectly good scam on a naive and unsuspecting real estate agent, and she takes on a young stud as an apprentice. Just another stumbling block in my path to fortune."

"Have you crossed paths with the young man?"

"In a manner of speaking."

"You exchanged words?"

"Not really."

"What does that mean?"

"I might have cursed at him when he cut me off in the parking lot."

"Ever stab him with a knife?"

"Is that a suggestion? It's not bad."

"He ever stab you?"

"I think I'd have noticed that. What are you getting at, Cora?"

"Someone left a bloody hunting knife under Johnny's pillow."

"Like in *The Godfather*?"

"That was a horse's head."

"Same idea."

"Not really. No one was trying to frame the guy for murder with a horse."

"You think someone's trying to frame this

guy for murder?"

"That's one idea."

"Wouldn't you need a dead body first?" Melvin threw back the rest of his scotch. "I wish you hadn't quit drinking. You were so much easier to get into bed."

"As if that were ever a problem."

"You're saying it's not?"

"I was married to you, Melvin. Surely you remember. It was back when you were dating that young blonde."

"Why rehash old times?"

"You started it."

"How did I start it?"

"With your sexy horsehead talk."

Melvin grimaced. "Just when I thought you were going to say something sweet, you go for the wisecrack."

"Unfortunately, I have to keep at arm's length with you, Melvin."

"Why?"

"Because I don't know what you're up to. You show up in town, a bloody knife pops up, and a crossword puzzle disappears."

"Crossword puzzle?"

"The sister of the kid with the bloody knife. Someone stole her crossword puzzle."

"And I care about this why?"

"It's another reason you're not getting me into bed."

"You just said that to be mean."

"How well you know me. So, that would be a no on did you stab Johnny."

"That would be a neat trick with him finding the knife under his pillow."

"It would. On the other hand, I couldn't rule out Johnny stabbing you until you showed up alive and breathing. Should I be fearing for the health of Judy Douglas Knauer?"

"Not unless she marries the young punk. As it is, he's just after her money."

"As opposed to you, whose motives are pure."

"I'm not going to cost her money. I'm going to make her money. Every piece of real estate I turn over she gets exactly the same thing as if she did it herself. I just get a little bonus that affects her not in the least. It won't even be reflected in the lease."

"Or on your tax return?"

"I can't afford to pay taxes. I'd have to stop your alimony payments."

Melvin cocked his head at Cora and smiled. "If you figure out who got stabbed, give me a call."

CHAPTER 13

Chief Harper called Cora at three in the morning. "Found the corpse."

"How come you always find 'em at three in the morning? What's wrong with three in the afternoon?"

"I'd have preferred that myself."

"Who got stabbed?"

"Fred Winkler."

"Who's Fred Winkler?"

"Guy who got stabbed."

"You just trying to make sure I'm awake, Chief? Don't bother. You had me at 'corpse.' Where's the body?"

"Middle of Main Street."

"Are you kidding me?"

"Wish I were."

"Never mind, I'll see for myself."

Cora slammed down the phone and hopped out of bed. Her clothes were scattered on the floor. It was not lost on her they hadn't been scattered by an ardent lover but by herself while watching a sitcom.

Buddy, the toy poodle, went out the front door, peed, and came back in. He knew what three a.m. meant.

Cora drove downtown, where Officer Sam Brogan was directing traffic with a flashlight. He started to wave Cora off, then recognized her and pointed to a parking spot in front of the police station. Cora pulled up and got out.

Chief Harper was in the middle of the street inspecting the body. Sam Brogan was protecting him with the flashlight.

The officer was cranky, as usual. "How can you have a crime scene in the middle of Main Street? You can't close off Main Street. It's Main Street."

"There's no traffic, Sam."

"No, but there will be, won't there? Just because you beat the ambulance doesn't mean it's not coming. Those boys don't care about anything. They'd drive right over the body if you'd let 'em."

The dead man lay facedown in the middle of the street. He wore blue jeans and a work shirt. He had what might well have been a knife wound in the middle of his back. His shirt was slashed and stained with blood. He was young, in his twenties, with short dark hair and a three-day-growth look that had become popular on television. His face was scrunched up against the pavement, and his neck was twisted in what would have been an exceedingly uncomfortable angle had the man been alive.

"That's Fred Winkler?" Cora said.

Chief Harper rose from the body. "According to his driver's license."

"How'd he wind up in the middle of Main Street?"

"Someone must have dumped him. I can't imagine anyone walking there this time of night. I can't imagine anyone dumping him there, either. Right outside the police station. Kind of a slap in the face."

"I doubt if that's why someone did it."

"Killed him, no. Dumped him, maybe. I mean, you wanna dump a guy, there's a lot better places with a lot less chance of being seen. Dumping him there is kind of sticking it to us."

A Volkswagen pulled up and Dr. Barney Nathan got out. Despite the hour, he was dressed in his traditional red bow tie. Cora had never seen him without it, except during their brief affair. She had actually worn it once, and not much else.

"What have we got here?" Barney said.

"I'd say it's a stabbing victim, but you're the doctor."

"Damned if I'm not." Barney knelt by the body. "Looks like a stabbing. No murder weapon?"

"No, we got one."

"You sent if off already?"

"I sent it off this afternoon."

Barney Nathan cocked his head. "If the guy had been lying here since this afternoon, surely someone would have noticed."

"He wasn't. Sam Brogan found him on his last drive-through."

"When was that?"

"About a half hour ago."

"He's been dead longer than that."

"You mind not telling Cora? She'll probably wind up working for the defense attorney."

"Well, I like that," Cora said.

Harper put up his hand. "Not that I care. The time of death will be public knowledge."

"I don't recognize him. Who is he?"

"Probably from that construction crew out at the mall. Most of them are from out of town."

"Was he?"

"More than likely. His driver's license is from New York. And he had a motel key in his pocket."

"Oh. Which motel was he staying at?"
"The one out by the mall."

CHAPTER 14

Cora Felton found Melvin enjoying a breakfast beer at the Country Kitchen.

"Little early for that, Melvin?"

"It is," he admitted. "I was thinking I should have a Bloody Mary, but then I figured what the hell."

"You find getting liquored up helps you sell houses?"

"The houses sell themselves. It's quite a racket, really."

"Fred Winkler."

"What about him?"

"You didn't happen to stick a knife in him and drop him in the middle of Main Street?"

"Can't say as I have."

"You mind letting me look in the trunk of your car?"

"For what, bloodstains? Be my guest."

"Right, you'd use a plastic tarp, wouldn't you?"

"I would hope so. Not that I've ever disposed of a body, but if I were going to do it, I'd like to do it right. Who's this guy you say?"

"Fred Winkler."

"Doesn't ring a bell."

"Young guy, brown hair, unshaven, work clothes."

Melvin shrugged. "There's a bunch of construction workers at the motel. He could be one of those."

"He certainly could, seeing as how he had a key to one of the motel rooms in his pocket."

"Good, they're a noisy lot. I'll be glad to see 'em go. You don't suppose he could knock off a few more, while he's at it?"

"Who?"

"Johnny Dawson. Wasn't he the guy running around with the bloody knife?"

"He wasn't running around."

"Sitting, standing, he's the guy who had it."

"He turned it in to the police."

"Bad move. I'd have told him to ditch it."

"He turned it in way before the murder. The knife will prove he's innocent."

"Really?" Melvin's grin was mocking. "He's way too young for you, Cora."

Cora's mouth fell open. "I have no designs

on Johnny Dawson."

"So you say. Would you like to know the number of times you said the same thing about some other lover you were seeing?"

"Johnny Dawson is not my lover."

"Isn't that a Michael Jackson song? When you start quoting lyrics, you're usually lying. If the guy means nothing to you, why are you defending him?"

"How about the fact he didn't do it?"

"Your evidence he didn't do it is the fact he had a bloody knife? You *claim* that was before the murder. So what was the time of death?"

"The police don't have a time of death yet."

"Isn't the doctor sweet on you? Why don't you give him a call and find out?"

"The doctor's barely talking to me, Melvin. If he could move out of town, I think he would. You, on the other hand, show up in town and dog my footsteps."

"Hey, I'm just sitting here. *You* came and found *me.*"

"To ask you if you killed someone. That's entirely different."

"Well, if you want to split hairs." Melvin took a gulp of beer. "When'd you find this out, Cora?"

"Three in the morning."

"You should have knocked on my door. Then you could prove I was there."

"He wasn't killed at three in the morning, Melvin."

"When was he dumped?"

"Probably around two, two thirty."

"You should have knocked on my door then."

"The body hadn't been found."

"Who said anything about the body?"

Out the window of the bar Cora could see the Channel 8 news van heading for town.

"What?" Melvin said.

"You might want to steer clear of town."

"Why?"

"TV's here."

"So?"

"What about your paranoid fear of publicity? Based on the premise that someone you scammed will see you on TV and come after you."

"A stupid notion. I'm surprised you bought that."

"I beg your pardon."

"I didn't want some bimbo I dumped to catch up with me. You know what a problem that is? Women really should learn to take a hint."

"I took a hint, Melvin. I can't speak for anyone else."

71

"Well, I'm not hiding from anyone. This might be a good opportunity to extol the benefits of Bakerhaven living."

"Sure. You can play up the trendy Murder of the Month Club. Too bad he was staying at the motel. You could have another vacant house on the market."

"Damned if I couldn't."

Melvin chugged the rest of his beer and hurried out. He hopped in his car and headed back to town.

Cora followed along to see if he really was looking to be interviewed.

He certainly wasn't lacking opportunities. Rick Reed and his camera crew had taken up positions outside the police station to nab anyone who came by.

Not wanting to be nabbed, Cora hung back in the crowd the TV cameras had created. Melvin, on the other hand, appeared to be positioning himself toward the front of the crowd, ready to be singled out. He gave every indication that if Rick Reed didn't call on him, he was going to volunteer.

Before he got a chance, Dan Finley drove up in his police car. He got out and opened the back door for Johnny Dawson. Johnny wasn't in handcuffs, but he might as well have been. Dan took him by the arm and marched him to the police station.

Rick Reed fell all over himself trying to get an interview, but Dan was having none of it. He ushered Johnny up the front steps and in the door.

Cora slipped out of the crowd and hurried down the side alley to Becky's office.

"They arrested Johnny Dawson!"

Becky looked up from her desk. "Oh, come on."

"Just now. I saw Dan Finley haul him in."

"That's a big mistake."

"No kidding. That knife can't have anything to do with it. They'll find that out as soon as they get the autopsy report."

"Unless they already got the report."

"Not a chance. If I were you, I'd get my fanny down to the police station before the poor sap spills his guts."

"I'm not his lawyer."

"No, but you could be. I bet if you showed up there, he'd hire you."

"I'm not soliciting employment. Good God, next thing you'll have me ambulance chasing."

"I hear there's good money in it."

The phone rang.

Becky scooped it up. "Becky Baldwin . . . Uh huh . . . Uh huh . . . Sit tight, I'll be right there."

Becky hung up the phone and smiled at Cora. "Guess who wants a lawyer?"

Chapter 15

"I don't see why I need a lawyer."

Becky Baldwin might have pointed out that she was there only because he had asked for her, so on some level Peggy's brother must have felt he needed a lawyer. Instead she applied the Socratic method. "You were arrested?"

"Yes."

"They said you didn't have to answer their questions?"

"That's right."

"So you decided not to say anything."

"Not at first. I was perfectly happy to talk to them as long as they believed me."

"What made you think they didn't believe you?"

"They started asking things I'd already told them."

"Did you point that out to them?"

"Sure."

"What did they say?"

" 'Tell me again.' "

"What sort of things did they ask you?"

"They said, 'When you picked up the knife, did you pick it up by the blade or the handle?' I said, 'The handle.' They said, 'Why?' I said, 'Because the blade was covered in blood.' They said, 'If the blade wasn't covered in blood, you would have picked it up by the blade?' I said, 'No.' They said, 'Then why did you say the reason you picked it up by the handle was that the blade was covered with blood?' I said, 'Because you asked the question.' They said, 'You're not supposed to give us the answers you think we want to hear, you're supposed to tell us what happened.' "

"What did you say to that?"

"I didn't say anything. It wasn't a question."

"What happened then?"

"They said, 'Is there anything else you told us you got wrong?' I said, 'I didn't get anything wrong.' They said, 'Then you did pick it up by the handle because the blade was covered in blood?' "

"And that's when you decided you wanted a lawyer?"

"That's right."

"I can't believe Chief Harper would question you like that."

"It wasn't him. It was a little guy with a twitchy nose."

"Henry Firth. I see."

"Who's Henry Firth?"

"The county prosecutor. He's the one who'll be trying the case if they charge you with the crime."

"Why would they charge me with the crime? I didn't do anything."

"You had the murder weapon."

"That's not the murder weapon."

"How do you know?"

"It couldn't be."

"It actually could. We don't know when this man was killed. Until we get the autopsy report, there's nothing to rule it out."

"When do we get the autopsy report?"

"The police will get it soon. If they don't already have it. They're not apt to share it with us."

"Don't they have to?"

"They do if they charge you with the crime. They haven't done that yet."

"That's good, isn't it? They must realize it wasn't the knife."

"Or they realize it was and they don't want us to know."

"What's the point of that?"

"No point. It's just a game they play."

"This isn't a game. I'm a murder suspect."

"Don't worry," Becky said, getting up from the table. "You won't be for long."

CHAPTER 16

Becky stormed out of the interrogation room. "Charge him or release him!"

"Hey, hey, hey," Chief Harper said. "Don't bite me. I'm just doing my job."

"Does your job include holding people in custody for no apparent reason?"

"Your client was in possession of a bloody knife."

"Which he immediately turned over to the police as soon as it was discovered."

"Which would be the smart move."

"Really? I would think the smart move would be to toss it in the river. If it was indeed the murder weapon. And if he was indeed guilty. Neither of which happens to be true."

"You know that because your client told you so?"

"I know that because I'm a rational human being and rely on facts. You, on the other hand, rely on pure conjecture. You see a bloody knife and assume it's a murder weapon."

"The presence of a stabbing victim does up the odds."

"The knife had nothing to do with it."

"Preliminary tests have not ruled it out."

"That's because they're so preliminary as to be next to worthless. It's way too early for a DNA match. I imagine your preliminary tests have indicated the presence of blood on the knife. You might even have gone so far as to match the type to the victim's. If it's type O, that's not an earth-shaking revelation, since it would match half the town. But I imagine Henry Firth is hoping I'll plead him out on the basis of it."

Chief Harper made a face.

Becky smiled. "Ah. I gather you were present for Henry's interrogation."

"Now look —"

Becky held up her hand. "I don't want to put you in a bad position, Chief. You're not about to say anything negative about the county prosecutor, but really. My client has given me a fairly detailed summary of the Q and A. Henry couched his questions in a way that fairly screamed for the young man to demand a lawyer. It was something along the lines of a have-you-stopped-beating-your-wife? interrogation."

"It wasn't that bad."

"How bad was it? Never mind, I know the answer. In a case with virtually no evidence, Henry's done everything he could to make the suspect look guilty in the event he ends up trying him someday."

Chief Harper said nothing.

"And what about the autopsy report? Hasn't the time of death ruled out the knife as the murder weapon?"

"Barney hasn't finished his report yet."

"Surely he has the time of death."

"He's not going to give you something you can cross-examine him on in court. He has to be sure."

"I'm not asking you for something I can use in court. I'm asking you to give me a hint."

"I can't give you a hint."

"Why not?"

"You're the defendant's attorney."

"Defendant? Then you *are* charging him with the crime?"

"I'm just trying to make it through the morning without everybody mad at me. If I tell you something, the prosecutor's mad at me. If I don't tell you something, you're mad at me. I got Rick Reed setting up shop outside just waiting for an exclusive interview with the chief of police. I got nothing to give him, but that won't stop him from pretending like I did. I can say no comment and he'll take it to mean we have the suspect dead to rights and he can expect a confession any moment. I swear to you, by tonight people will be talking as if I said it. I don't care as long as it's just folks, but when it's the county prosecutor I want to be able to say I didn't say it. And that goes double for what I didn't say to you. So there is absolutely nothing I can tell you about the time of death. Do you understand me?"

"Perfectly."

CHAPTER 17

Cora Felton walked up to the receptionist in Barney Nathan's waiting room and said, "Please tell the doctor I love him."

Heads turned. The patients on the couch pricked up their ears. Born gossips, this was too good to be true.

The receptionist looked like she'd swallowed her gum. "I beg your pardon?"

"Tell Barney I want to see him. I'm sure he wants to see me. If he doesn't, tell him I will stand up every ten minutes and loudly proclaim my affection until he changes his mind or his wife shows up."

The receptionist blanched, shot to her feet, and disappeared through the door to the examining room. She was back a minute later with the nurse, who walked up to Cora and said with a frosty smile, "The doctor will see you now."

Neither of the patients on the couch objected to Cora being taken first. They wouldn't have missed this for the world.

The nurse ushered Cora into Barney's office. "The doctor will be with you in a minute."

"I certainly hope so," Cora said. "I'd hate to bust in on him with a patient."

Barney Nathan was in a minute later. His face was almost a red as his bow tie. "What the devil do you think you're doing?" he said.

"Hi, Barney. I wanted to talk to you."

"So you stood up in the middle of my waiting room and said you loved me?"

"There were a lot of patients ahead of me. I didn't want to wait."

"So you chose to humiliate me?"

"Sorry, Barney, but you were being a bit of a horse's ass."

"How dare you!"

"Come on, Barney, you know I dare just about anything. I'm working for Becky Baldwin. She'd like to get the autopsy report that you've been withholding at the request of the police."

"I haven't been withholding the autopsy report."

"Of course not. So when Chief Harper says you haven't finished your autopsy, that's because you took time out in the middle to see a few patients."

"Now, look here —"

"Barney, I know how it is. Henry Firth likes to play games. But he can't play them with the medical profession."

"I have never altered a report."

"Altered it, no. Withheld it . . ." Cora waggled her hand. "The medical finding exonerates Becky's client. As soon as it's presented, the cops will have to let him go. So Henry doesn't want it presented. But that's not his decision. Johnny Dawson is not going to be tried for this crime, but in the event he is, you know how much mileage Becky Baldwin will get out of this little game? Particularly when she refreshes your recollection about this conversation. I'm sure the two patients in the waiting room will be eager to lay the foundation. So pick up the phone and tell Chief Harper the time of death, so we can all go about our business."

Barney didn't want to do it, but the longer he waited, the worse it would get. He reached for the phone.

"Atta boy," Cora said.

CHAPTER 18

Cora got back to the police station just in time to see Johnny going out the door and Melvin going in.

"Hi, honey, I'm home," Melvin said as he went by in handcuffs. "You mind calling that pretty little lawyer you work for and telling her I might be needing her services? It seems the police think I killed someone."

"Fred Winkler?"

"I assume that's the guy. Apparently they were just waiting for a time of death to arrest me, and wouldn't you know it, the doc came through."

"Becky may have a conflict of interest."

"She always has a conflict of interest. She'd love to get me off, but she's afraid I'll hit on her. That's silly. I'll hit on her in any case. Explain it to her, will you?"

"Don't say anything until you talk to Becky."

"I can't take her advice if she's not my

lawyer."

"She'll get you a lawyer."

"From New York? I'll grow old waiting. I'll hang myself in my cell."

Rick Reed, gleefully filming the exchange for Channel 8, tried to jump in. "Officer Finley, is this man a suspect in the murder of Fred Winkler?"

"Get him inside, Dan. I've got this one." As the door closed behind Dan and Melvin, Cora said, "It is way too early to speculate on what this all means, Rick. But I promise to keep you up to date as soon as we know more."

Cora hurried down the side street and up the stairs to Becky's office. She burst in right on the heels of Johnny Dawson.

"Hey, guys, no time for amenities. The cops let Johnny go on the basis of the autopsy report I got Barney Nathan to release. They've arrested Melvin on the basis of God knows what, so he'll probably blame me for the autopsy report. He wants to hire you as his lawyer. I pointed out the conflict of interest, told him you'd either resolve it or find him another lawyer."

Cora flopped down in a client's chair and put her feet up.

"You look pleased with yourself," Becky said.

"Hey, it's not every day you can strong-arm a medical examiner and get your ex-husband arrested. Not that I had anything to do with that, but Melvin's gonna give me the credit."

"What do they have on him?"

"I have no idea. But, hey, it's a murder case. So why don't you finish up your case with Johnny and see if it precludes you from taking this one. Seeing as how I cost you a client, I'd kind of like to get you another."

Johnny was looking back and forth from one to the other. "Hey, you guys are having a lot of fun, but I just got out of jail. Would you mind telling what the hell is going on?"

"It would appear you're in the clear. The doctor's put the time of death after you turned in the knife. So without even waiting for DNA tests, we can prove it's not the murder weapon."

"And that's it," Becky said. "Unless you can think of some further reason you require my services, our business is done. You gave me a hundred-dollar retainer. There will be no further charge."

"Uh huh," Johnny said. Cora couldn't tell if he was delighted at being charged so little, or if he felt Becky hadn't done any work and didn't deserve to be paid.

"Then you have no objection if I represent

someone else in this matter?"

"Not if the cops have cleared me."

"They have," Cora said.

"Are you sure?"

"Arresting someone else for the crime is a pretty good sign," Becky said.

"If you get him off, will they arrest me again?"

"Good point," Cora said. "This young man has a fine legal mind."

At the look on Johnny's face, Becky said, "Oh, for goodness' sakes, tell him you're kidding, will you?"

"Fine. I'm kidding. You're off the hook. Run along and let her try to get the next guy off. Trust me, it's going to be a lot harder."

"What do the police have on him?"

"I have no idea."

"Then how do you know?"

"I was married to him."

CHAPTER 19

Becky walked into the police station to find Chief Harper conferring with Dan Finley.

"I hear you have a suspect in the Fred Winkler case."

"We do," Chief Harper said. "Were you thinking of representing him?"

"It crossed my mind."

"Could you do me a favor and try not to get him released before happy hour. Rick Reed is starting to refer to our revolving-door policy."

"I can't help it if you keep arresting innocent men."

"This one might not be innocent."

"Hold the phone. Let me get Rick Reed in on this. Chief Harper thinks the latest suspect he arrested just might actually be guilty."

"Do you happen to know any different?"

"I have no idea about the disposition of

90

this case. I haven't even heard the suspect's story."

"When you do," Chief Harper said, "don't take it at face value until you've heard mine."

"What's your story?"

"Oh."

Dan Finley grinned. "Walked into that one, didn't you, Chief?"

"Yes, yes," Harper said impatiently. "None of us are going to tell each other anything. Anyway, I'd appreciate a modicum of restraint. Turning Cora loose on the doctor wasn't particularly subtle."

"I had nothing to do with that."

"Isn't she your investigator?"

"And do you think she looks to me for guidance? Asks me if I approve her shenanigans?"

"No, I don't. On the other hand, we have a sensitive situation here."

"Why is that?"

"The suspect happens to be her ex-husband."

"So? It's not like there's any love lost between them."

"No, but there is a bond of animosity."

"That's well said, Chief. I think Cora would appreciate that."

"She doesn't have to stand up and cheer.

I'd be happy if she didn't storm the police station."

"She was here when he was brought in. Did she storm the police station then? No, she just told me he was here."

"And you stormed the police station."

"I dropped by to see the prisoner. I understand he's requested a lawyer. Are you saying I shouldn't have come?"

"You're not going to win this one, Chief," Dan Finley said.

"Well, you don't have to look so pleased about it." Harper sighed. "All right, go tell him his lawyer's here."

CHAPTER 20

Becky sized up Melvin across the table in the interrogation room. She realized he was sizing her up at the same time. And not necessarily as a lawyer.

"Hi, Becky. It's good to see you."

"There must be easier ways of attracting my attention."

"I thought of just dropping in, but you're so standoffish. Did you know that? Anyway, I do much better with a purpose. A stated purpose, I mean."

"I know exactly what you mean. So, what did you do now?"

"What makes you think I did something?"

"You got arrested."

"That's not really my fault."

"Whose fault is it?"

"Don't be like that."

"Why did the police arrest you?"

"They obviously made a mistake."

"Obviously. What led them to make this

mistake?"

"Stupidity, I imagine."

"Melvin."

"Why do they think I did it? I don't know. They haven't told me."

"What did they tell you?"

"Nothing. They just asked me questions. When I asked for a lawyer, that ended the conversation."

"Why did you ask for a lawyer?"

"I wanted to see you. It's been awhile, you know."

"Stop being delightfully unhelpful. Why do you think the police arrested you? What could possibly connect you to the crime?"

"I knew the victim."

"How did you know the victim?"

"Apparently, we were staying at the same motel."

"You didn't know that?"

"No."

"How'd you find out?"

"The cops said so."

"You recognized his name?"

"They showed me his picture."

"Was he alive in the photo?"

"He was dead. Didn't look much worse than usual, if you ask me."

"So you knew him by sight but not by name. How did you know him?"

"There's a roadside bar just south of the mall. Guys hang out there after work."

"Including you?"

"Yeah. Why?"

"Hard to imagine you doing any work."

"That's unkind. Just because my work isn't necessarily the nine-to-five type."

"Or any other legitimate type."

Melvin smiled in a way Becky was sure he considered irresistible to women.

"Anyway, you hung out in the bar, you met Fred Winkler."

"It wasn't so much that I met him."

"What was it, then?"

"He took offense."

"About what."

"He was hitting on a waitress. She couldn't have liked it. It was disgusting. I told him to knock it off."

"This is a waitress you were hitting on?"

" 'Hitting on' is such a nasty term. Chatting her up sounds so much better."

"When did you ever care how something sounded?"

"I wouldn't want you to get a bad impression of me."

"It's a little late for that, Melvin."

"That's just unkind."

"So, when you told him to knock it off, he apologized and went back to drinking with

95

his friends?"

"Not exactly."

"What did he do?"

"He put his hand on my chest and pushed."

"And you apologized and went back to drinking alone?"

"I may have pushed back."

"Even though he was young enough to be your grandson."

"I wasn't picking on a two-year-old. This was a big, strapping man."

"That's what I implied."

"I'm not that old, Becky."

"You're not that young, either. Do those hair plugs really fool anyone?"

"They don't have to fool anyone. They just have to look good. You've seen the girls I've been with."

"I have. I think I babysat some of them."

"If you get me out of here, we could discuss that over drinks."

"I'm trying to get you out of here, Melvin. You seem more interested in being cute than cooperative."

"I'm trying to cooperate. I just don't know anything. The victim and I had an altercation in a bar. It didn't amount to much. He tried to push me around. He found out he couldn't. He put his hand on my chest. I put him in an arm lock and offered to break his wrist. He seemed rather surprised, but he backed right down."

"Did this impress the waitress?"

"Not in the way I hoped. The bartender suggested we knock it off or leave."

"So there are several witnesses to this altercation."

"I'm sure there are."

"Still, it's not enough to pick you up. They must have something else."

"I can't imagine what it is."

"That's the only contact you had with the victim?"

"That's right."

"I thought you said you were at the same motel."

"We were."

"How do you know that?"

"I saw him there."

"So you had contact with him."

"No, I just saw him in passing."

"And you, being the shy, retiring type, lowered your eyes and walked the other way."

Melvin merely smiled.

"Was this before or after the barroom incident?"

"I believe it was after."

"Don't kid me, Melvin. You'd know."

"It was after."

"What happened?"

"He was with some of his friends. When they saw me, two of them stepped in front of him."

"And?"

"I laughed. He tried to get at me. They held him back."

"It never got physical?"

"Only when I mentioned his mother."

"Melvin!"

"It was nothing. He took a swing at me and I broke his nose."

"You're kidding!"

"No, that was it. I gave him a bloody nose, and he slunk away licking his wounds."

"Great," Becky said dryly. "And there were how many witnesses to this encounter?"

"Two or three. I'm not sure."

Becky thought that over. "Well, it's bad, but it's not enough. They must have something else."

"Like what?"

"Like a witness who saw you dumping the body in the middle of the street."

"I doubt it. I was very careful."

"Don't even joke about it. You have anyone who can account for your whereabouts last night?"

"I'm afraid not."

"I find it hard to believe you came up here without a bimbo in tow."

"Maybe I just wanted to see you."

"Meaning I'm a bimbo?"

"Hardly. You're true blue."

"What's that make Cora?"

"You're jealous? That's sweet."

Becky left Melvin in the interrogation room and hunted up Chief Harper.

"Charge him or release him."

"Fine. I'll charge him."

"Why?"

"You just told me to."

"You got nothing on him, Chief."

"I got more than you think."

"You mind telling me what?"

"I would mind. Henry Firth would have a cow."

"Henry Firth can tell me himself, unless he wants to stipulate my client can be released on his own recognizance."

Chief Harper shook his head. "Sorry. You're going to have to schedule a bail hearing."

"Why so hard-nosed?"

"This is not a speeding ticket, Becky. This is a murder."

"This is a murder that has nothing to do with my client."

"Henry Firth sees things differently."

"Henry Firth doesn't see anything at all. Henry Firth is embarrassed about having arrested one suspect and having to let him go. So he picks up a second one as a buffer. What he doesn't realize is that letting the second one go is going to be *way* worse than the first one. And denying bail is just the icing on the cake. Judge Hobbs will grant it, I'll post it, and Melvin will walk. All insisting on the hearing does is give Rick Reed time to set up."

Becky jerked her thumb at the desk. "Mind if I use your phone?"

"Be my guest."

Becky called the courthouse. "Judge Hobbs? . . . Really? Well, could you have him call me. I wanna post bail for Melvin Crabtree."

CHAPTER 21

Becky found Cora hanging around outside Cushman's Bake Shop with a latte and a scone.

"Second of the day?" Becky said.

"Third, but who's counting. Of course, my day started at three in the morning."

"Right."

"What are you so upset about?"

"Does it show?"

"You look like you caught your boyfriend in bed with twin Pilates instructors."

"That happened to you?"

"They might not have been twins. So what's wrong?"

"Melvin didn't like the decedent."

"Of course not. He's male. Did he know him?"

"They had an argument in a bar."

"Let me guess."

"That's right. Over a girl. The waitress, no

less. There were many witnesses to the alter-cation."

"If Melvin killed every guy he fought with over a girl, it would alter the census."

"He also broke his nose."

"Same fight?"

"No, and there's witnesses to that, too.

"Par for the course. What else have they got?"

"That's the thing. I have no idea. But it must be something, because I can't get him released."

"What?"

"Henry Firth is insisting on a bail hear-ing. Judge Hobbs is out to lunch, so I can't get Melvin out."

"What's that all about?"

"That's what I'd like to know. Usually it's a courtesy thing. I ask that he be released on his own recognizance, and Henry says okay because he knows I'll make sure he shows up. Even so, we ought to be able to agree to a number, I'd post it, and that would be that. But Henry doesn't even want to talk to me. He says take it to court, and Judge Hobbs is out to lunch. What do you think that means?"

"He probably was hungry."

"They gotta have something more to

prove it than the fact Johnny Dawson didn't."

"Melvin's a loudmouth. You have no idea what he said in that bar."

"I can imagine, but I'm not happy. This is strange behavior, even for Henry Firth. Picking Melvin up is one thing. Charging him is another. Charging him and haggling over bail is damn near unprecedented. We gotta go in front of the judge, the media's in town, and the bail hearing will get reported. If the cops don't have anything, Henry Firth is going to be very red in the face."

"Ah. The Case of the Red-Faced Rat. Sounds like a Perry Mason mystery."

Becky's cell phone rang. She clicked it on. "Hello? . . . Oh, hi, Henry . . . I'd like that, but Judge Hobbs is out to lunch. Is this really necessary? I mean, how much are you asking? . . . I'm not asking you to show your hand. What the hell does that mean? Fine. See you then."

Becky clicked the phone off in disgust.

"What's the score?" Cora said.

"We have a bail hearing at three."

"Three?"

"Yeah."

"Just in time for all the news outlets to be alerted."

"Yeah."

"That's strange," Cora said. "It's almost like he *wants* the news outlets to be alerted."

"It sure is."

CHAPTER 22

Judge Hobbs surveyed the crowded court-room with displeasure. "This is a simple bail hearing. There is no reason for anyone to be here."

"I'm willing to go, Your Honor," Melvin said brightly.

"So I understand. Let's see if we can accommodate you. Mr. Prosecutor, what do we have here?"

"This is Melvin Crabtree, charged with homicide in the stabbing death of Fred Winkler. The State is asking that bail be denied and the defendant be remanded to custody."

Becky's mouth fell open. "Your Honor, that's outrageous. I've never heard of such a thing. The prosecution has no reason to hold my client. I ask that he be released on his own recognizance."

"Those would appear to be opposing points of view," Judge Hobbs said dryly. "Have opposing counsel attempted to effect a compromise?"

"Opposing counsel didn't want to talk about it and demanded a bail hearing. I didn't realize they were intending highway robbery."

"That will do, Ms. Baldwin. I realize there are spectators in the courtroom. Please don't play to them."

"Yes, Your Honor. But I was prepared for a bail hearing, not an ambush. The prosecutor gave no indication he intended to push for no bail."

"I thought you hadn't discussed this with the prosecutor."

"Exactly, Your Honor. I tried to discuss it with him and was told he wanted a bail hearing. Until I got here, I had no idea why."

"Well, now we do. Let's get on with it. Mr. Firth, why are you pushing for no bail?"

"The defendant is a flight risk, Your Honor. He is not a resident of Bakerhaven. He is not even a resident of Connecticut. If he is released on bail, there is every reason to believe he will leave the state, if not the country."

"Nonsense, Your Honor. It's not as if Mr. Crabtree has no ties to the community. He is employed by the real estate broker Judy Douglas Knauer, and he is the ex-husband of Cora Felton, a long-time Bakerhaven resident. Moreover, he has nothing to fear from prosecution, as the charges against him are groundless. He has no incentive to run."

"Not so, Your Honor. Mr. Crabtree had a personal animosity against the victim. Witnesses can attest to two separate physical encounters within the last week, one in a roadside bar and one outside the motel where he and the victim both were staying. In one instance, Mr. Crabtree broke the decedent's nose, and the only thing that kept him from doing more serious bodily harm was the fact that other people intervened."

"It's a far cry from a barroom brawl to stabbing a man in cold blood," Becky said. "If the prosecutor would like to amend the charge to drunk and disorderly, I'm sure we could work something out."

Judge Hobbs put up his hand. "No need to respond, Mr. Firth. The court takes judicial cognizance of your unwillingness to amend."

"I hope the court also takes judicial cognizance of the fact the level of proof offered by the county prosecutor is insufficient to even charge my client with murder, let alone ask that he be held without bail."

"I quite agree," Henry Firth said. "And if that was all I had we would not be standing here. But Your Honor will recall issuing a search warrant earlier today. Following up on that warrant, Officer Dan Finley of the Bakerhaven police department inspected the rental car of the defendant, which he located in the parking lot of the Country Kitchen restaurant. The search uncovered a hunting knife stained with blood. Preliminary tests show the blood to be the same type as the decedent's, and DNA tests are under way to prove that it is indeed blood from the victim. In light of such incontrovertible evidence, I find it highly likely the defendant might attempt to flee."

Rick Reed filmed gleefully as the court went wild.

CHAPTER 23

Judge Hobbs nearly broke his gavel pounding for order. Finally he gave up and ordered the courtroom cleared. It took some time. No one was prepared for trouble at a simple bail hearing, but Dan Finley and Sam Brogan leapt into the breach, assisting the court officer in carrying out the judge's instructions.

When order was finally restored, Becky Baldwin said, "Your Honor, I strongly object to these wildly inflammatory statements on the part of the prosecutor, remarks that would seem aimed solely for the media."

"You said the defendant had no reason to flee," Henry Firth said. "I was merely refuting your statement."

"In the most inflammatory language possible."

"You're not objecting to the facts, just the way they were presented?"

109

Judge Hobbs banged the gavel. "That will do."

"I would point out this is not a probable cause hearing, we are merely requesting bail," Becky said.

"That's because we *have* probable cause, Your Honor," Henry Firth said. "If we did not, opposing counsel would be jumping up and down *insisting* on a probable cause hearing."

"Be that as it may," Judge Hobbs said. "The court is inclined to schedule a probable cause hearing when the results of the DNA test are in. In light of the current situation, I find the defendant has sufficient motivation to fear prosecution."

"Oh, Your Honor," Becky said.

Judge Hobbs waved her down. "On the other hand, to keep him incarcerated pending the results of such tests would be considered harsh. These things drag on, despite how much one attempts to expedite them. All that is necessary here is to assure that the defendant show up for trial. I therefore set bail in the amount of five hundred thousand dollars."

Becky nearly gagged. "A half a million dollars, Your Honor? Where do you expect the defendant to come up with that type of money? Even a bail bond would cost my client fifty thousand dollars. And that's not refundable. Why should a man be forced to pay that type of money to get out of jail for a crime he didn't commit?"

"You make it sound like I'm binding him over on a whim. The alleged murder weapon was found in your client's car. That is hardly the fault of the court."

"If it was placed there by someone else, it is hardly the fault of my client. The decedent's quote 'friends' unquote were aware of the hostility between the two men. If one of them found himself in possession of a bloody knife, what better place to dispose of it than the defendant's car?"

"This is not the time to argue the merits of the case," Judge Hobbs said. "We are merely setting bail."

"Bail is not meant to be punitive. It is only to assure the defendant shows up in court."

"You need not lecture me on bail."

"I can't post bail for my client in such a staggering amount, and I can't let him remain in jail."

"I can post bail, Your Honor," Melvin said.
Becky stared at him.

Judge Hobbs was so startled he didn't even comment on the irregularity of the interruption. "I beg your pardon?"

"I'll post bail. The full amount, not a bail

111

bond. Then there's no problem with me forfeiting ten percent. Unless the court takes a ten percent service charge."

Judge Hobbs's eyes narrowed. "If you're joking, you are out of line. If you're not joking, you are in contempt. Cash bail will be returned in full, as you well know. You claim you can post it?"

"I don't have a half a million on me, Your Honor. Will the court take a check?"

"A certified check would be fine. The defendant is remanded to custody until he has posted bail."

"Your Honor," Melvin said. "We seem to be getting into a catch-22 situation here. I can't arrange for the check if I'm in jail."

Judge Hobbs glared at the prisoner. "You seem to be having too much fun. This is a serious matter and a very serious charge."

"I understand, Your Honor."

"The defendant is remanded into custody pending bail."

Judge Hobbs banged the gavel and stalked out of court.

CHAPTER 24

"You can post a half a million dollars' bail?"

"Well, I don't want to stay in jail."

"Where did you get that kind of money?"

"I don't believe that's relevant to the current situation."

"If the money was illegally obtained, it certainly is. If I knowingly post bond with tainted money, I am liable to prosecution."

"Don't do it, then."

"Don't post bail?"

"Don't knowingly post tainted money. You don't know my money's tainted. I don't see what the problem is."

Cora bustled up. "Where the hell did you get half a million dollars?"

Melvin grinned. "Hi, Cora."

"Were you just showing off? Judge Hobbs isn't going to find it very funny. He takes a dim view of people who make a mockery of his court."

"I know. I've seen you in action."

"I didn't mean me. He likes me."

Becky coughed discreetly.

Dan Finley appeared at Melvin's elbow. "Okay, let's go. If you promise not to run, we can forgo the handcuffs. They make phoning and check writing rather difficult."

"Ladies, you wanna lecture me later? Right now I'm at the mercy of the court. I'll drop by your office once I've posted bail. Maybe I can take you out to dinner."

"She's not interested, Melvin," Cora said.

"I can speak for myself," Becky said.

"You tell her," Melvin said. "No reason to miss dinner just because she's jealous."

"I'm not jealous, Melvin. I'm just looking out for a friend."

"I love it when you girls fight over me. Well, see you soon."

Dan Finley led Melvin away.

"You think he's really got it?" Becky said.

"Not unless he knocked off a bank."

"What if he posts bail with stolen money?"

"You'll be in the clear because you didn't know it. The point isn't whether the money's tainted. The point is whether he has it."

"Why?"

"He pays me alimony. Never mind he's often late. If he's got a bunch of money he's been concealing, we should go back to court."

"For God's sakes, Cora. The man's accused of murder and you want to hit him with an alimony suit?"

"Why not? He didn't kill anyone, but he sure cheated on his wife. I'd have gotten a lot bigger bucks if he hadn't pleaded hardship. It's tough to plead hardship with half a million bucks. How long do you think it will take him to post bail?"

"Might be a little while."

"And then he's going up to your office?"

"That's what he said. Why, you wanna be there?"

"Hell, no."

CHAPTER 25

Cora pulled into the Stop & Shop out at the mall and drove around to the back. She was in luck. A bunch of cardboard boxes in fairly good condition were lying next to the Dumpster. She took half a dozen of the cleaner ones, threw them in the backseat of her Toyota, and drove out to the motel. She grabbed one of the boxes as a prop and went up to the office.

Cora adopted what she felt was an appropriately subdued tone. "Hi. I'm here to pack up the decedent."

The manager was glad to see her. Cora figured he would be. With the construction crews in town, he was short on space and happy to get the room back. He didn't even ask her who authorized her to pack up, which was a good thing since no one had. She just needed an excuse to go to the motel.

"Guy's roommate moved out," the manager said. "That's never good. With two guys, one of them will usually pay. But when one moves out, you don't know if he's the money man or just along for the free ride."

"Don't they pay in advance?"

"They do, a week at a time. At the end of a week they have to go or pay. With a rented room, if a guy wants to be a jerk, it's bad."

"What do you do?"

"Wait till he goes out, then change the lock."

"Sounds effective."

"It is. But it's hard to check in guests while a tenant is throwing a fit. You lock someone out, he's apt to say a few unkind things about the motel."

"I can imagine," Cora said.

"Anyway, the guy's dead, and I lose the money. And the guy who killed him was staying here, too, so now I'm out two rentals."

"The other guy didn't kill him. His lawyer's getting him released now."

"He'll be coming back? That might not be good for business. What if his friends make trouble?"

"You know Fred Winkler's friends?"

"I don't know 'em. They rent rooms. Nothing wrong with that, as long as there's no trouble. With their friend gone, there'll be less."

"Fred Winkler was a troublemaker?"

"I heard there was an altercation. I didn't see it, but I heard."

"Well, I'll get his things out for you. You got a passkey?"

"I can't give you that, but I can open the door. Just don't lock yourself out until you leave."

It didn't take long to pack up Fred Winkler's things. The man had been traveling with a single suitcase. Cora plopped it on the bed, filled it with the clean clothes from the dresser drawers and the dirty clothes that were scattered willy-nilly around the room.

Everything else she threw in the cardboard box. There were toiletries from the bathroom, a girlie mag from the bedside table, and a collection of beer bottles, mostly empty. Cora left them for the maid.

The ashtrays were clean. Whatever vices he might have had, Fred Winkler did not smoke. There was no motel safe. Everything Fred Winkler had was out in the open.

He had a backpack with a few incidentals. A Swiss Army knife, opposed to the hunting knife that killed him. A spiral notebook, some pencils with broken points, some ballpoint pens, sixty-seven cents in change, and a couple of pills of dubious origin: one, a green-and-white capsule that had half the powder missing; the other a white tablet covered with dust and hair.

There was a windbreaker hanging in the closet. Cora crammed it and the backpack into the cardboard box.

Leaving the door to the unit wide open, Cora carried the box and the suitcase out to the car, stashed them on the backseat, and walked back into the unit.

She waited two beats, came out the door, and walked down to unit 12.

Cora had broken into motel rooms before. She had once climbed in a bathroom window. She had once climbed *out* a bathroom window, but that was another story.

She marched up and banged on the door. There was no answer. Melvin was downtown bailing himself out of jail, but she wanted to make sure she hadn't gotten the room number wrong and was about to break in on some amorous couple.

Cora was in no mood for subtleties. She reached into her floppy drawstring purse and pulled out her gun. She didn't shoot the lock off, however, she merely smashed a pane in the front window.

She snaked her hand in, groped for the door. The doorknob was just within reach.

She fumbled around with her fingers, clicked the lock.

The last time Cora had searched Melvin's motel room, there had been a bimbo involved. It was kind of weird to be doing it when there wasn't.

From habit, Cora bent down and looked under the bed. While she was at it, she checked under the mattress. There was nothing there.

Recalling *No Country for Old Men,* she stood on a chair and unscrewed the cover of the heating vent near the ceiling. There was nothing hidden in the duct. There was not even a string to pull out whatever might have been hidden around the bend. Cora could have told that just from unscrewing the old cover. It hadn't been disturbed in years.

Melvin had a briefcase. That, she knew, was a charade, just another prop to make him look like a real estate broker, or whatever other businessman he was representing. In the course of normal events, Melvin would rather have been shot dead than caught carrying a briefcase. It gave the impression he was employed, which detracted from the rich playboy image he worked so hard to cultivate.

Cora riffled through the papers in the

briefcase. As she expected, they were meaningless gobbledygook, intended merely to confuse and confound. A person confronted with them would either be incredibly impressed or realize they were dealing with a fraud.

Cora flipped through the pages and stopped dead.

It was a standard boilerplate contract from a major publishing company. Cora recognized it instantly. She had signed a number of them herself for the lucrative series of Sudoku books that were published in her name.

The amount of the contract, $800,000, leapt off the page. So did the name Melvin Crabtree, typed in the blank marked "Author."

That answered the question of how he was able to post bail. The man had a six-figure book advance.

The contract was for a work of nonfiction of approximately seventy-five thousand words.

The work was tentatively titled *Confessions of a Trophy Husband: My Life with the Puzzle Lady.*

CHAPTER 26

Cora got home to find her niece Sherry and Sherry's daughter, Jennifer, doing the laundry. Jennifer loved helping Mommy, particularly transferring the clothes from the washer to the dryer. Cotton socks made wonderful wet balls, which Jennifer could wind up and pitch right through the door of the front-loading dryer.

Jennifer had started the game as a toddler, standing right in front of the dryer, but as she grew older and more proficient, she had gradually backed up farther and farther until now, as a first grader, or what she herself referred to as a big girl, she could get eight out of ten from all the way across the room.

Sherry was not entirely pleased, as that meant two out of ten socks wound up on the floor, but Cora, who had grown up in an age when girls weren't allowed to play ball, couldn't wait for Jennifer to be old enough for Little League.

As Cora came in, a rolled-up sock sailed across the room, bounced off the top of the dryer, and plopped to a soggy stop on the floor.

"She's working on her knuckle curve," Sherry said. "Whose fault do you suppose that is?"

Cora waved it away. "Yeah, yeah, yeah. Let her practice. I need to talk to you."

Jennifer had been gung-ho before, but since she had been to Yankee Stadium she was irrepressible. "I wanna show Auntie Cora!" she squealed.

"Show me two times. Auntie Cora has to talk to Mommy."

Jennifer threw two pitches. Unfortunately, she missed the second one and insisted on trying again. The first she got right down the middle. The second was high and outside.

"Again!" Jennifer cried.

"Uh oh," Cora said. "She's prolonging the game. A bad habit to get into. Jennifer, if you throw two in a row you can have ice cream."

"Ice cream!"

"She doesn't have ice cream before dinner," Sherry said.

"It's a special occasion," Cora said. "If I

123

don't talk to you, I'll go mad. You want ice cream, Jennifer?"

"Ice cream!" Jennifer whooped and hurled two socks into the dryer.

"Perfect," Cora said. "Get your ice cream."

Jennifer squealed and raced out of the laundry room.

"You can't let her serve herself," Sherry said. "She'll eat a whole half gallon."

"Let her. We got trouble."

"Can't it wait five minutes?" Sherry said.

"No," Cora insisted, but Sherry was already out the door.

In the kitchen, Jennifer was about to plunge her spoon into a full pint of Häagen-Dazs chocolate chocolate chip. Sherry intercepted it, set a bowl on the table, and spooned out a reasonable portion.

"More!" Jennifer cried.

"That's plenty," Sherry said.

Jennifer made the most adorable face. "Little more?"

"How can you resist that?" Cora said.

"I have a lot of practice," Sherry said. She portioned out one more spoonful into Jennifer's bowl and put the ice cream back in the freezer. She was about to lecture Jennifer on the virtues of moderation when Cora dragged her out of the kitchen.

"What's so damn important?" Sherry said.

"Melvin wrote a book."

"What?"

"At least he's writing one. He has a six-figure contract with a major publisher. *Confessions of a Trophy Husband: My Life with the Puzzle Lady.*"

Sherry sank down in a chair. "Oh, my God," she murmured.

"Exactly."

"This is a disaster."

"That's what I've been trying to tell you."

"Does he know you know?"

"Not yet."

"Are you going to tell him?"

"Not if I can help it."

"How'd you find out?"

"I saw his contract."

"How did that happen?"

"Well, that's the problem."

"Uh oh."

"Yeah."

"Where was the contract?"

"In his briefcase."

"Where was his briefcase?"

"In his motel room."

"You broke into his motel room?"

"Kind of."

"Does he know it?"

"He might infer it."

"How?"

"From the broken window."

"Cora, you've got to stop doing these things."

"What things? Sherry, you're missing the big picture here. Melvin's writing a book about me. The fact that I broke into his motel room is entirely coincidental."

"I'm not sure Chief Harper will feel that way."

"So what are we going to do?"

"Short of killing him?"

"Let's not rule out any options."

"Cora."

"Well, I'm not going to remarry him, if that's what you're thinking."

"God forbid. What if you offered to forgive his alimony?"

"That would be good if it ran to eight hundred thousand dollars. Otherwise he's not going to be impressed."

"Eight hundred thousand dollars?"

"Apparently, I'm a big sell."

"For that money they're not looking for a happy puff piece."

"No, they're going to want every salacious tidbit. Trust me, Melvin's got 'em."

"What's the worst they can be?"

"I have no idea. If you'll recall, I was drinking fairly heavily then. What I can remember would ruin my image. What I can't remember would probably land me in jail."

"It can't be as bad as all that."

"We're talking Melvin. He brought a date to our wedding."

"You didn't object?"

"I didn't know till the wedding night. I wondered why he was plying me with champagne."

"Stories like that will kill us. We'll lose our sponsor for sure. Granville Grains will not consider that a wholesome image for schoolchildren."

"That's nothing," Cora said. "He can hit me with every morals charge from here to Sunday. We could weather that." She grimaced. "But he's going to expose me as a fraud."

"He wouldn't do that."

"Why not?"

"It kills the goose that lays the golden eggs."

"Yeah, but they're *our* golden eggs. For eight hundred thousand bucks he's not going to care. He'll throw everything in the book but the kitchen sink." Cora's eyes widened. "Oh, that miserable bastard!"

"What?"

"He took a selfie with me in front of the

coffee shop. You wanna bet it's for the book?"

"How are we going to stop him?"

"I could frame him for murder."

"Isn't he already framed for murder?"

"Yeah, but it isn't going to stick. I could manipulate a little evidence."

"What evidence?"

"I don't know. But I'm his lawyer's investigator. I'm bound to come up with something."

"You're supposed to come up with something that *helps* him. That's what you're paid for."

"Well, if you want to nitpick."

"Seriously, how are we going to handle this?"

Cora shook her head. "We may not be able to. It may be all over. We have to start thinking about our second lives. You as the Puzzle Lady. And me as the Puzzle Lady impersonator."

"Don't even joke about it."

"That's not a joke. If Melvin blows the whistle, we're screwed. What's going to stop him?"

"So how do you want to play it?"

"I want to stall. That's all we've got going for us. I should sign a few contracts of my own, get some Sudoku books in the works, maybe squeeze in a few Granville Grains commercials."

"Isn't that worse?"

"What?"

"Doing commercials when you *know* you'll be exposed? If you take Granville Grains' money for commercials knowing they'll be worthless — isn't there a special penalty for that?"

"I probably get my own circle in hell." Cora shrugged. "What's the difference? It's not like I go directly to jail. Or hand over all my ill-gotten gains. It would take complicated legal procedures to sort it all out. Which fits right into my philosophy. Stall, stall, stall."

"What about Becky?"

"What about her?"

"Did Melvin tell Becky?"

"I'm a fraud?"

"Yeah."

Becky knew Cora couldn't solve crossword puzzles but still thought she constructed them. That was not as impossible a concept as it sounded. Noted cruciverbalist Harvey Beerbaum believed the same thing.

"I don't know," Cora said.

"Better find out."

"She might not tell me."

"How could she possibly keep it from you?"

"If it was a confidential communication from her client, she might be bound to keep it from me."

"Oh, come on, Cora. As if you couldn't tell."

"How? By asking probing questions? By making her suspicious, if she's not already?"

"Give me a break. If this was anything else, you wouldn't be arguing with me. You'd be falling all over yourself to do it. You'd bust into her office, haul Melvin out of his chair, slap him around a few times, and say, 'All right, guys, what's up?' "

"That's not much of a plan."

"Well, it's better than busting in on me and feeding Jennifer a half a pint of ice cream before dinner."

"It wasn't half a pint."

"It's before dinner. Once you breach that sacred barrier . . ."

"It's a special occasion. Kids understand special occasions."

"What special occasion?"

"I'll make one up."

"Cora."

"Trust me. How bad can it be?"

Jennifer ran out of the kitchen waving a spoon. She had chocolate ice cream all over

130

her face, down the front of her dress, and in her hair.

Buddy was yapping at her heels and licking up the drops of melted ice cream that fell from the spoon. The poodle had evidently licked her bowl clean. He was wearing a chocolate bib.

Jennifer spun in a circle, sending a shower of chocolate drops in every direction, offered her most beguiling smile, and said, "Buddy wants a little more."

CHAPTER 27

Cora burst into Becky's office, where the young attorney was conferring with her client. "All right, you guys. What the hell is going on?"

"I'm having a confidential conversation with my client. I wasn't planning on broadcasting it to the world."

"You think I'm going to tell Rick Reed?" Cora flopped into a chair next to Melvin. "Relax. I was married to Melvin during some of his darkest hours. Did I ever rat you out to the cops?"

"Well, actually —" Melvin said.

"Oh, shut up," Cora said. "I'm talking serious stuff. I may have had you arrested now and then, but that was normal husband-wife business. Practically foreplay."

"Do I need to be here for this?" Becky said.

"I don't know. What has Melvin told you?"

"You know exactly what Melvin's told me.

He didn't do it, and someone stuck a knife in his car."

"Someone also stuck a knife in Fred Winkler. You know anything about that, Melvin?"

"I didn't see it happen, if that's what you mean."

"Who would have a reason to frame you for this crime?"

"Hey," Becky said. "Who's the attorney here? I know you two are in love, but —"

Melvin and Cora reacted at once.

"In love?" Cora thundered.

Melvin laughed derisively. "Are you kidding me?"

Cora turned on him. "Well, I like that. You scoff at the idea?"

"Don't you?"

"Of course. But not in a hurtful way. There's no reason to be rude about it. There was a time we meant something to each other."

"Yes. I believe your attorney explored that time during the alimony hearing."

"Why dwell on the past, Melvin? There is this current situation."

"Exactly," Becky said. "If you wouldn't mind coming back to earth, I would like to know why I'm suddenly deluged with a rash of clients framed with bloody knives."

133

"Unless I find one in my Toyota, let's assume that run is over," Cora said. "I'm all for finding out how Melvin got his. Unless he'd prefer another investigator on the case. One with whom he does not have so much history."

"You want to prove my innocence, feel free," Melvin said. "Just don't expect me to help you. I know absolutely nothing about the situation."

"How about where you parked your car?"

"It was in front of the Country Kitchen."

"All night?"

"No, when they picked me up. I was having lunch."

"I saw you there," Cora said. "That was the first time you denied killing Fred Winkler. And just where was the knife discovered?"

"Apparently in the glove compartment."

"Did you happen to look in your glove compartment when you started your car?"

"No. Why would I do that?"

"I don't know, but it would pin down the time. The knife was planted last night or this morning. Which is more likely?"

"Neither is more likely. It simply makes no sense."

"Then why would the police search your car?" Cora looked at Becky. "That's the hundred-dollar question, isn't it?"

"It wasn't an illegal search," Becky said. "They had a warrant."

"How the hell did they get a warrant?"

"Based on allegation and belief."

"What the hell does that mean?"

"I don't know. It's the sort of thing lawyers say."

"Becky."

"The cops had a warrant. I can demand a probable cause hearing and find out on what basis they got a warrant, but if they aren't inclined to tell me, I'm not likely to find out."

"Don't you have back-channel sources?"

"What do you mean, back-channel sources?"

"Put on something slinky and ask Dan Finley."

"He's impervious to my charms."

"Nonsense," Melvin said. "There's not a man alive impervious to your charms."

"Not even gay ones?" Cora said.

"Her allure defies demographics."

"Pretty flowery language, Melvin. You getting all highbrow on us?"

"I'm actually educated. You just never saw that side of me. I'm maturing into an upright citizen."

"Who's working a real estate scam and

charged with murder."

"There's no stigma attached to that. Any man may be charged."

"Most of them don't bloody the victim's nose and keep the murder weapon in their glove compartment."

"I'm as surprised as you are."

"Okay, kids," Becky said. "I hate to interrupt, but we do have this murder to deal with. Could the two of you stop bickering and concentrate on that?"

"Of course," Cora said. "Pay attention, Melvin." She smiled at Becky. "You have our undivided attention."

Peggy Dawson burst into the office waving a piece of paper. "I found the puzzle!"

CHAPTER 28

Melvin plastered on his most ingratiating smile. "And who is this fine young lady?"

"Oh, for God's sakes, Melvin," Cora said. "She's twelve."

Peggy's eyes blazed. "I am not!"

"Of course not, sweetheart. You have to forgive these people. They're a little tense because I've been charged with murder. I suppose you've heard about it?"

"I should think so, Melvin," Cora said. "Her brother was also charged."

"Oh, is he your brother?" Melvin said. "Well, don't worry. I won't hold it against you. We can't choose our relatives."

Peggy giggled. "You're funny."

Cora's eyes widened. "No, no, no, no. He's *not* funny. Trust me on this. Ignore him and focus on the subject. Where'd you find the puzzle?"

"In Johnny's room."

"In Johnny's room?"

"Yes."

"Why'd you look there?"

"Because he didn't."

"He did look there. That's where he found the knife."

"Yes," Peggy said. "He found the knife and stopped looking. I mean, is he really going to look for a puzzle after a bloody knife?"

Cora frowned.

"Of course not," Peggy said. "He finds the knife, he calls the police. You and the officer come out and get it. So I figured he stopped looking. And I figured right. There it was, in his bottom dresser drawer."

"The puzzle was in plain sight in his bottom dresser drawer?"

"Well, if you opened the drawer."

"It was on top of his clothes?"

"Not exactly."

"What does that mean?"

"It was under his clothes."

"So if you lifted up his clothes, the puzzle was in plain sight."

"You're making fun of me. Why are you making fun of me? I looked for it and I found it. I think I did well."

"I think you did superbly," Melvin said. "Let me see the puzzle."

Peggy passed it over.

Across

1 Was decked out in
5 Some roll-call votes
9 Paint layers
14 Haley of "Roots" fame
15 Eye leeringly
16 How an actor may enter
17 Start of a message

19 Midler of "The Rose"
20 Makes certain
21 Aromatherapy spot
23 Elemental ending
24 "Cool" amount of money
25 "Not to mention . . ."
27 Greets the day
30 More of the message
35 Nile slitherer
36 Suffix with home or farm
37 Ferber who wrote "Show Boat"
38 Escalator segment
40 Fritter away
41 Pointillist's marks
42 Slightly, in music
43 Take in or let out
44 Cut, as a branch
45 More of the message
47 Drinks quickly
49 Apollo's instrument
50 Place off limits
51 LAX guesstimate
53 Mdse.
55 Midsummer Classic player
59 Pirate's pal
61 End of the message
63 Worth a 10, say
64 Legs, in old slang
65 Enthralled with
66 There's no accounting for it

67 Ring stoppages, for short
68 Consider to be

Down

1 Enjoy the kiddie pool
2 Ken of "Brothers & Sisters"
3 Chianti and cabernet
4 Dig up
5 Sing in the Alps
6 Swelled heads
7 "Aladdin" prince
8 Gets firm
9 Deep blue
10 Talc's value on the Mohs scale
11 G.I. Joe, e.g.
12 "Swan Lake" wear
13 Outwardly appear
18 Dwarf planet beyond Pluto
22 Cater to a voting bloc, say
26 Depot posting, informally
27 Like Satchmo's voice
28 Playground rejoinder to "Ain't!"
29 Makes risky investments
30 Lake Como's locale
31 Villa _____ (estate in 30-Down)
32 "Them" novelist Joyce Carol
   _____
33 At the summit
34 Makers of paper nests

141

36 Moved to the music
39 Small bouquet
46 Sock pattern
47 Guys' partners
48 Implied, perhaps
50 Grace word
51 Send out
52 Bit of verbal fanfare
54 USAF E-5
55 Shells, but not ziti
56 Daly of "Cagney & Lacey"
57 Start the kitty
58 Part of a Clue board
60 Chow down
62 Cask material

"It looks okay to me," Melvin said. He cocked his head at Cora. "Of course, *I* don't solve these things."

Cora's smile dripped venom. "I'm surprised, Melvin. You have so many other talents."

"We all have things we're good at," Melvin said. "Solving puzzles doesn't happen to be mine."

"But it is yours," Peggy said, picking up the cue and looking at Cora. "Please. It's important now. Solve the puzzle for me."

"What makes you think it's important now?" Cora said.

"A man is dead. And my brother was accused of killing him. Because he had a knife where the puzzle should have been. And it turns out the knife wasn't the murder weapon. So my brother is innocent, except he had the puzzle. And how did that happen? It seems to me, that's gotta be important."

"That's because you're not accused of murder, dear. Ask Melvin if he thinks it's important."

Melvin opened his mouth.

"No, don't ask Melvin. He'll say it's important just to be contrary, but in point of fact, it isn't. It's an unimportant puzzle, and as such it is handled in the way we handle all unimportant puzzles." Cora grabbed the puzzle from Melvin, thrust it out at Peggy. "Take it to Harvey Beerbaum."

"But —"

"Let him solve it. If it says anything significant, it's a clue. As it is, it's just wastepaper."

"That's a pretty dismissive attitude, considering your ex-husband's on trial for murder," Melvin said.

Peggy stared at Cora. "You were married to him?"

"Cut me a break, kid," Cora said. "I was young and foolish once."

"Wow." Peggy looked Cora up and down. "Must have been a long time ago."

CHAPTER 29

Harvey Beerbaum wasn't pleased to see Peggy again. He'd been reluctant to enter her house, and he was even less inclined to let her into his. Not that she gave him much choice. She pushed right by him the minute he opened the door.

"Now see here, young lady," Harvey said, but she was long gone, ignoring him completely and looking around the living room as if it were the wing of a museum.

"Oh, what a cute house!" Peggy said.

Harvey Beerbaum's house was cute in that it was decorated with crossword puzzle memorabilia. There were trophies from his finishes in various crossword puzzle tournaments. Harvey had never won one, but he had finished as high as third in various regional tournaments, and in the top ten in one of the national ones. There was a crossword puzzle cuckoo clock, a crossword puzzle lava lamp, and a crossword puzzle dartboard. There was a wooden stand with a large crossword puzzle grid on which the finalists had once competed, a relic from American Crossword Tournaments gone by. And there were framed photos of Harvey at the tournament posing with the likes of Will Shortz and the late great Merl Reagle.

"I'm glad you like it," Harvey said. "Now, if you could wait outside."

"I have the puzzle for you. The one we couldn't find. I found it."

"That's wonderful. Now, if you'd take it outside —"

Peggy plunked herself down at the kitchen table. Though Harvey lived alone, it was set for four, perhaps to show off his crossword puzzle place mats. She pushed the plate aside and flopped the puzzle down on the mat.

"Now see here —" Harvey began.

Peggy pulled a pencil out of her pocket and thrust it in his face. "Here you go. Solve it."

"We can do this outside," Harvey said.

"Why? You got a table right here. Outside you got nothing to lean on. The pencil will go right through the paper. You can't do that."

Harvey heaved a huge sigh. It would be faster to do the puzzle here than physically remove her. Safer, too. It would be hard to evict her without touching her, and the minute he did that, he was in the soup. He'd be labeled a sex offender for the rest of his life. It was either solve the puzzle or run screaming out the door. It was almost a toss-up.

Harvey sat at the table and solved the puzzle as fast as he could. Fear was an amazing impetus. At that rate, he might have actually won the tournament.

Peggy grabbed for the puzzle. "What does it say? What does it say?"

Harvey wasn't about to fight her for it. He left it on the table, rose from his chair. "See for yourself."

She snatched it up, peered at it. "So? What's the answer?"

"Read the theme entry."

"What's the theme entry?"

"Give it back."

"Why?"

"So I can read it."

"You just wrote it."

"I just solved it."

"Don't you have to read it to solve it?"

"Not the same way."

Harvey held out his hand. If she didn't hand it over, he was going to walk out the door. But she did.

147

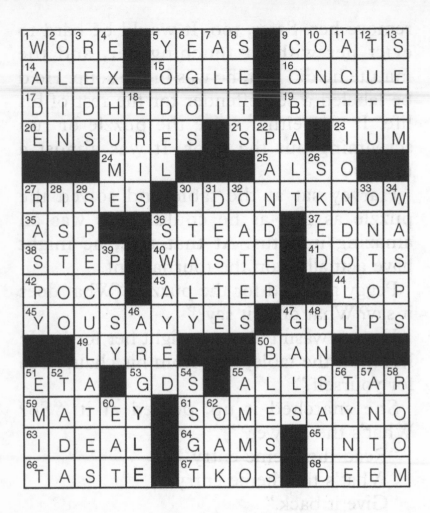

The completed crossword grid:

W¹	O²	R³	E⁴		Y⁵	E⁶	A⁷	S⁸		C⁹	O¹⁰	A¹¹	T¹²	S¹³
A¹⁴	L	E	X		O¹⁵	G	L	E		O¹⁶	N	C	U	E
D¹⁷	I	D	H	E¹⁸	D	O	I	T		B¹⁹	E	T	T	E
E²⁰	N	S	U	R	E	S		S²¹	P²²	A		I²³	U	M
			M²⁴	I	L			A²⁵	L	S²⁶	O			
R²⁷	I²⁸	S²⁹	E	S		I³⁰	D³¹	O³²	N	T	K	N	O³³	W³⁴
A³⁵	S	P		S³⁶	T	E	A	D		E³⁷	D	N	A	
S³⁸	T	E	P³⁹	W⁴⁰	A	S	T	E		D⁴¹	O	T	S	
P⁴²	O	C	O	A⁴³	L	T	E	R		L⁴⁴	O	P		
Y⁴⁵	O	U	S⁴⁶	A	Y	Y	E	S		G⁴⁷	U⁴⁸	L	P	S
		L⁴⁹	Y	R	E			B⁵⁰	A	N				
E⁵¹	T⁵²	A		G⁵³	D	S⁵⁴		A⁵⁵	L	L	S	T⁵⁶	A⁵⁷	R⁵⁸
M⁵⁹	A	T	E⁶⁰	Y		S⁶¹	O⁶²	M	E	S	A	Y	N	O
I⁶³	D	E	A	L		G⁶⁴	A	M	S		I⁶⁵	N	T	O
T⁶⁶	A	S	T	E		T⁶⁷	K	O	S		D⁶⁸	E	E	M

"What does it say? What does it say?" Peggy cried.

Harvey read the theme entry aloud:

"DID HE DO IT?
I DON'T KNOW
YOU SAY YES
SOME SAY NO."

148

Peggy's mouth fell open. "Oh, my God!"

"What?"

"This is about the murder."

"How could it be about the murder?"

"It is! It is! How could it mean anything else? There's been a murder, and a man's been accused."

"Yes, but —"

Peggy grabbed Harvey's pudgy face and kissed him right on the lips.

Horrified, mortified, and blushing bright pink, Harvey sat in stunned silence as Peggy grabbed the puzzle and darted out the door.

CHAPTER 30

"He solved it! He solved it!" Peggy cried, crashing into Becky's office.

"I'm sure he did," Cora said. "And I'm sure he regards it as every bit an achievement in the annals of crossword puzzle lore as you do. But to some of us it is not a momentous event. So if you wouldn't mind flying out the door as quickly as you came in we'll be able to go about our business."

"You don't understand. He solved the puzzle and it's a clue."

"Unless it's a clue that has something to do with the murder, I'm not interested," Becky said. "Cora, would you mind taking your protégé outside?"

Cora bristled and rolled her eyes. Between being kidded about her ex-husband and being kidded about Peggy Dawson, she was ready to bite someone's head off. Not having had any sleep might have been a contributing factor.

"Give me the damn puzzle and let's get on with it."

"Here." Peggy shoved it into her hands.

Cora took the puzzle, read the answer. " 'Did he do it? I don't know. You say yes. Some say no.' " She slapped herself on the forehead. "Oh, my God! It's perfectly clear. It's practically a confession. Sorry, Melvin, it looks like you're done for. Better hunt up Ratface and see if we can plea-bargain."

Peggy was not too young to know when she was being mocked. "Hey," she said, "this is serious."

"I'm glad you think so," Cora said. "I hate to spoil your fun, but I feel constrained to point out you got this puzzle *before* the murder, so whoever is equivocating about whoever's guilt or innocence can't *possibly* be referring to that."

"Oh, no? What if they'd already plotted the murder? What about that? What if this was all part of the killer's plan? What if the killer says, 'I'm going to kill this guy, and in order to get away with it, I'm going to frame someone for it? I'll write a crossword puzzle that makes him look guilty. So you all will think it's him. Then I'll take the murder weapon and plant it on him to finish the job'?"

Melvin smiled. "You've got a good head

151

on your shoulders, young lady. But I don't think anyone would write a crossword puzzle about me."

Peggy pointed at Cora. "*She* would. What if she wanted to frame you for the crime? She sends me a crossword puzzle, knowing I'll bring it to her. She doesn't want to solve it herself, since she's the one who made it, so she sends me to Harvey what's-his-face to solve it, knowing I'll bring it back. Since Harvey's the one who solved it, no one will think she's involved."

Melvin grinned at Cora. "You sure she's not your clone? She has a really convoluted mind."

Cora turned to Becky. "I can't tell you how sorry I am about all this."

"Why are *you* apologizing?"

"I don't know. This case has me batty. So what do you want to do with this crossword puzzle?"

"I suppose we should give it to Chief Harper," Becky said.

"That's right," Peggy said. "Give it to the cops!"

"He's not going to be happy," Cora said.

"Are you happy?" Becky said.

"Hell, no."

"Then why should he be any different?"

CHAPTER 31

Chief Harper scowled. "You're bringing me a crossword puzzle?"

"That's right."

"It has something to do with the murder?"

"I doubt it very much."

"Then why are you bringing it to me?"

"So you can't say I didn't."

"You paying me back for arresting Melvin?"

"This has nothing to do with your arresting Melvin. I have no problem with your arresting Melvin. You can arrest Melvin as much as you like. That pain-in-the-ass Dawson girl insists this has something to do with the murder. I don't think so. Becky doesn't think so. You won't think so. So you can read it, and file it, and you'll never hear about it again, but no one can give you any grief that you didn't. See how it works, Chief? It's a win-win."

"Then why do I feel like I just bought the

153

Brooklyn Bridge?"

"Have you even seen the Brooklyn Bridge, Chief? It's not a bad buy."

Chief Harper took the puzzle, looked it over. " 'Did he do it? I don't know. You say yes. Some say no.' " He looked at Cora. "This doesn't mean anything."

"Congratulations, Chief. Join the club. Your concurrence leaves Peggy Dawson in a minority of one. Just where you want to leave her. So now that's taken care of, you wanna discuss the crime?"

Chief Harper smiled and rubbed his hands together. "Ah. The ulterior motive. It's a relief to know you have one. By all means, let's file your silly crossword under hollow ruses and get to what you really came for."

"The crossword is what I came for, Chief. The chitchat's incidental."

"The fact your ex is accused of murder not withstanding?"

"I wonder how that happened."

"How what happened?"

"Melvin got accused of murder."

"Well, it wasn't on a whim. He happened to have the murder weapon."

"So he did, and that's very interesting. Because I happen to know Melvin. I know what he would and would not do. One thing he wouldn't do is get caught with the murder weapon. First, because he wouldn't commit a murder, and second, because it's stupid. The guy's committed a murder, so what does he do? Leaves the knife in his glove compartment and goes out to lunch."

"Killers often make mistakes."

"Oh, please don't give me that lame excuse cops always make when their logic doesn't make any sense. Yes, killers often make mistakes. They miss a fingerprint when they wipe off the gun. They don't realize they can be seen from a second-story window when they do the deed. Their alibi breaks down. These are the type of mistakes we're talking about. They don't make the mistake of behaving like a two-year-old who doesn't realize possession of the murder weapon might connect them to the crime."

"Stop spouting talking points. I agree possession of the murder weapon is open to other interpretations. Would you agree it's something that needs to be explained?"

"Absolutely. And if I find the person who put it there, I'll be sure to ask them. Let's not kid each other, Chief. No one's got the faintest idea what's going on. So it behooves us to find out. We can start by looking at what we know."

"What do we know?"

"We know the police found the knife in Melvin's glove compartment."

"Which you claim proves his innocence," Harper said sarcastically.

"Let's not go around again. All we know is the police found it there. And how did they find it there? They found it all nice and legal because they had a search warrant. And how did they get a search warrant?"

"Henry Firth went before the judge."

"And how did Ratface know to do that?"

"I beg your pardon?"

"You know exactly what I'm getting at. Did he do it on a hunch? Of course not. He wouldn't have thought to ask for it, and Judge Hobbs wouldn't have granted it. You asked for a warrant to search Melvin's car. Now, how'd you know to do that?"

"I can't discuss the case with you."

"Oh, *this* you can't discuss. We were discussing the case just fine, but this you can't discuss. Because Ratface is so obsessed with winning one he's playing games. We want to know on what basis a search warrant was obtained on our client. Are you really going to make us jump through legal hoops to do so?"

"I have to follow the instructions of the prosecutor. There are certain things I am not at liberty to say."

"For instance?"

"For instance, if the police obtained a warrant on the basis of an anonymous tip, I couldn't tell you."

Cora considered that. "This tip you couldn't tell me about — would that be a phone tip?"

"I couldn't tell you about any tip, but I particularly couldn't tell you about one on the phone. And I'll thank you to remember I didn't."

"That phone tip you can't tell me about — would that be a male voice or a female voice?"

"It's hard to say."

"Then don't. Hit me with a hypothetical. That'll protect you."

"I'm not even sure which hypothetical to postulate."

"Was the voice male or female?"

"That's hard to say."

"I know it is. That's why we're using hypotheticals."

"That's not what I mean."

"What do you mean?"

"Hypothetically, suppose the voice was androgynous?"

"Wow, Chief. Each time I think you've come up with your word for the day, you top yourself. Androgynous. What did this androgynous voice say?"

"Hypothetically?"

"Androgynously."

Harper grinned. "It's hard to stay mad at you."

"Oh, were you mad at me? What for?"

"I have no idea."

"Well, now that we're friends again, you wanna tell me what you have on my ex?"

"Aside from the murder weapon? He had a history with the decedent. A history of jealousy, rivalry, and violence. There are witnesses to these incidents, and none of them seem particularly disposed toward Melvin. We also lack a viable alternative suspect."

"You arrested one."

"He appeared to be in possession of the murder weapon. Turns out he wasn't."

"And wouldn't that be a wonderful way to convince you he didn't do it? Get himself arrested on the basis of evidence that proves to be false. It's enough to make you overlook any evidence that might possibly be true."

"What evidence?"

"Well, there you have me at a disadvantage. What other evidence have you got?"

"Now we've moved strictly into the realm of things that can help the defense. When you ask for chapter and verse of what Becky will claim constitutes reasonable doubt, we have overstepped the bounds of friendly discussion."

Cora shrugged. "Can't blame me for trying. Let's get back to the theoretical phone tip. I assume you traced the call?"

"You may theorize anything you like."

"With what result?"

"I don't know. Were I making such a call and didn't want it to be traced, I would probably use a burner phone and immediately destroy it."

"And that didn't make you suspicious of the tip?"

"There would be no reason to trace such a call until it had been checked out and borne fruit. At which point the murder weapon would have already been found."

"The alleged murder weapon."

"Of course."

"No, I mean it. That knife is alleged to be the murder weapon. You have yet to connect it to the victim."

"Wanna bet we can?"

"Not particularly."

"I don't blame you. Odds on it's a good bet. Framing him with a knife that isn't the murder weapon is sort of a hollow gesture."

"Someone did it to Johnny Dawson."

"Damned if they didn't. Now who would gain from that?"

"I give up. Who?"

"Someone who wanted to establish the fact that the possession of a so-called murder weapon did not necessarily constitute guilt."

"And people accuse *me* of being convoluted. You wanted to bet, Chief. Wanna bet on whether that's a theory the prosecutor chooses to advance?"

"Are we done discussing the crime? Because I'm running out of questions to ask you."

"Oh, is that what you thought we were doing?"

"I never thought anything else." Harper leaned in confidentially. "Seriously, Cora. Off the record. Did Melvin do it?"

Cora considered the proposition. She smiled and weighed the choices with her hands. "You say yes. Some say no."

She ducked out the door before he threw the puzzle at her.

CHAPTER 32

Melvin wasn't ducking the media. He walked out of Becky's office straight into the arms of Rick Reed.

"Mr. Crabtree! Mr. Crabtree! Rick Reed, Channel 8 News. Could I ask you a question?"

"You just did, Rick. The answer is yes."

Rick was momentarily taken aback, but he forged on. "Mr. Crabtree. You are the suspect in the stabbing death of the late Fred Winkler."

"The current suspect, Rick. They had someone else yesterday, and I'm sure they'll have someone else tomorrow."

"I'm glad you can take it so lightly."

"Well, I didn't do it, so it can't be all bad. The police made a mistake. I'm sure it will all get straightened out."

"Is it true you put up half a million dollars cash bail?"

"That's true, Rick."

"Why did you do that?"

"I believe in my innocence."

"Where did you get so much money?"

"I robbed a bank."

"You *what*?!"

"I hated to do it, but I had no choice. Half a million dollars is a lot of money."

"You're kidding me."

"I can't slip anything over on you."

"What *do* you know about this case?"

"Only that there *is* no case. Apparently someone planted a knife on me. I don't know why. It never would have occurred to me. But I'm not guilty of anything. Except maybe leaving my car unlocked."

"You claim someone put the knife in your car?"

"I not only claim it, I know it."

"How do you know it?"

"Because I didn't."

"Why would anyone frame you for murder?"

"I don't know. I'm not a famous person. On the other hand, I was married to the Puzzle Lady, who *is* a famous person. Perhaps someone wanted to get at her through me. If so, it would be a very clever way to do it. Particularly, if the killer wasn't good at crosswords."

"Why do you say that?"

"If the killer *was* good at crosswords, they could involve her by simply including one."

Cora Felton, who had come out of the police station in time to catch most of Melvin's interview, watched the spectacle with mounting horror. Before he was done, she reached a decision, tore herself away, and went up the steps to Becky's office.

"Melvin's on TV."

"Why am I not surprised? I assume he's giving Rick Reed an interview?"

"That's right. And you know why?"

"Because he's an egotistical idiot."

"Besides that."

"What do you mean?"

"He's promoting a book. That's where he got his bail money."

"Are you kidding me?"

"No, he got a huge advance."

"Who could possibly care about Melvin?"

"Think about it."

"Huh? Oh, my God!"

Cora nodded. "That's right. *Confessions of a Trophy Husband: My Life with the Puzzle Lady.*"

"Is he going to kill your career?"

"I have no idea."

"I suppose not. So he's going to get into all the sordid things you did when you were married."

163

"Hey, hey, give a girl a break. Just because you never tied the knot doesn't give you the right to be all high and mighty."

"I suppose I could have phrased that better."

"I'm sure Melvin can. At least, his ghost-writer will."

"Did Melvin tell you?"

"He doesn't know I know."

"Then how do you know?"

"I can't tell you."

"Why not?"

Cora made a face. "You're Melvin's lawyer. You have to act in his best interests."

"So?"

"If it's in his best interests to throw me under the bus, you've gotta do it."

"How is letting him know you know about a forthcoming book going to do that?"

"Well, it wouldn't hurt him, and that's all you care about. On the other hand, *not* letting him know I know about a forthcoming book wouldn't hurt him in the least. And not letting him know *you* know about his forthcoming book wouldn't hurt him, either. So is there any rule of law that says you have to tell your client everything you know when it makes no difference in terms of his best interests?"

"I think I followed some of that."

164

"Fine, we won't tell him. Now, does this new information alter his defense in any way?"

"I haven't even planned his defense."

"Good. Now you have this tidbit to keep in mind when you do. But as far as the actual subject, it won't come up unless Melvin raises it."

"Why are you telling me this now?"

"What do you mean?"

"You must have known for a while."

"Actually, not that long, but I take your point. I'm telling you now because I realized what Melvin's doing. He's promoting his book. He's not saying he wrote a book, but he's drumming up publicity for himself so when he does say he wrote a book, people will be interested. And whaddya wanna bet he includes a chapter about being a murder suspect?"

"Oh, hell."

"Anyway, someone tipped off the cops to search Melvin's car. He used a burner phone and trashed it, so we can't trace it that way. It was a neutral voice, could have been male or female."

"Where'd you get all that?"

"I'm the best."

"Seriously."

"I *didn't* get all that, and we can't let

165

anyone know I got all that, or we might get a police chief in trouble."

"I see," Becky said. "You know, there's not much about this case we can let anyone know."

"Right. As opposed to Melvin, who's spilling it all. I suppose it balances out. Anyway, I found out about the phone tip. It was an androgynous voice, might have been a man or a woman."

"That doesn't help us much."

"Actually, it does. If it was a man, he had a high voice."

"So we're not looking for James Earl Jones."

"I think we can rule him out. Luckily, we're in no hurry. Your client's out on bail, and life is good. I can stumble around in the dark without alerting anyone to what we know and see what I can come up with."

CHAPTER 33

Cora conjured up her most alluring smile. "Melvin, what's your game?"

"Game? No game. I'm just trying to survive this unfortunate fiasco."

"Why are you giving interviews on TV?"

"I project well, Cora. It's always been part of my charm. If this ridiculous case ever goes to trial, I'd appreciate some friends on the jury."

"Friends would have to disqualify themselves."

"As if. I doubt if they'd let any exgirlfriends on, but they can't object to someone just because they like me."

"You'd be surprised."

"Not much surprises me, Cora. I know the prosecutor can argue anything he wants, and I know Becky can argue anything she wants, and the truth doesn't even have to lie anywhere between the two. I assume you caught my interview?"

"Part of it."

"I thought I worked in some good promotion."

Cora nearly did a spit take. She and Melvin were having drinks at the Country Kitchen, and her Diet Coke went up her nose. She choked, coughed, got control of herself. "Promotion?" she said as casually as she could.

"For Judy Douglas Knauer. I made a nice pitch for affordable homes for sale or rent. I wouldn't be surprised if she makes a few sales."

Cora was relieved. So that was all he meant. "I'm sure there's nothing Judy wants more than the endorsement of a murder suspect."

"Hey, publicity's publicity. Anyway, just as soon as you get me off —"

"*I'm* going to get you off?"

He grinned devilishly. "You always could get me off."

"Oh, for God's sakes, Melvin."

"I'm counting on you to come up with the evidence that clears my name. Yes, the police found a knife, and, yes, it has blood on it, but that doesn't mean it's the murder weapon. The other guy's knife wasn't the murder weapon, so why should mine be?"

"Someone's is."

"In that case I vote for his."

"He turned it in before the murder, Melvin."

"Yeah, according to that doctor you used to sleep with. You think I'd take his word for anything? If he could slant the case against me, I have no doubt he would. Did they ever check the blood on Johnny's knife? Just because the time's wrong according to the doc, there's no reason to quit there. Find out if they matched the blood. For that matter, find out if they matched the blood on my knife. Just because someone's tying to frame me doesn't mean they've done a good job of it. I wouldn't put it past Johnny to put a knife in my glove compartment just to get himself off the hook. Whether it has anything to do with the murder or not."

"Now you just sound paranoid."

"Someone's trying to frame me for murder and I sound paranoid? If I didn't sound paranoid, there would be something seriously wrong with me."

"Who could tell? There *is* something seriously wrong with you."

"Granted, but indifference to my situation is not part of it. I didn't kill Fred Winkler, any knives in my glove compartment notwithstanding, and I would appreciate anything that demonstrates that fact."

"I'll see what I can do."

CHAPTER 34

"You get the tests back on the knife yet?"

Chief Harper looked up from his desk in irritation. "Can't you let a guy catch his breath?"

"Take a breath. Hell, take two. And tell me about the knife."

"It's way too early for the knife."

"Not Johnny's knife."

"You want to know about Johnny's knife?"

"Absolutely. You didn't throw it out just because you got another favorite suspect."

"That's not how we work."

"I'm glad to hear it. So what *did* you do with it?"

"It's being tested."

"Is it an essay test, or multiple choice? Some knives are not that sharp."

Harper groaned. "You didn't really say that."

"I didn't mean to. I just fell into it. Come on, Chief. You've had more than enough

171

time to test Johnny's knife."

"I'll call the lab."

"You can do that?"

"We have a phone."

Harper punched in the number. "Chief Harper, Bakerhaven. Looking for test results in the Fred Winkler case. I know it's too early to get the report, I'm just looking for something preliminary. Is Manny around? . . . Thanks." He covered the phone. "We're in luck. Manny's in the lab. If it was the other guy, we'd have to wait . . . Hi, Manny, I know you're not done. I'm just wondering about the knife . . . That's what I thought. What about the other one? . . . Yeah, the first knife. The doc ruled it out, I wondered if you did . . . That's what I thought. So how far along are you, when will you know? . . . Of course it's not for publication, you think I want to go out on a limb? Even if I weren't taking you with me? I just need a working hypothesis . . . Yes, I have to do it anyway, is there a reason you're busting my chops? I know you like to be thorough. I wouldn't want you to miss your golf game."

Harper laughed, put down the phone. "He hung up on me. How do you like that?"

"I prefer an answer."

"It's not Johnny's knife. I'm not giving

that out yet, but it's all right because nobody's going to ask. That knife's ruled out two ways, on time and blood type. So if Becky wants to bring it into court and make a big deal, I'm afraid she's out of luck."

"I'm sure that wasn't her intention."

"Of course not. That's why you asked."

"And Melvin's knife?"

"It probably is the murder weapon. Not only does nothing rule it out, but a lot of things rule it in. It's the decedent's blood type. We're still pending a DNA match, but Manny says we're going to get it. So it looks like it's Melvin's knife."

"Well, I would hope so," Cora said. "It would be rather pointless to frame him with a knife that wasn't the murder weapon."

"I know how you feel."

"I don't think you do. You've been married to one woman all your life, who I'm willing to bet has never been arrested for anything."

Dan Finley pushed through the front door, ushering in a young man in blue jeans and a dirty T-shirt. He had that rough-hewn sunburned look of someone who works outside.

Dan saw Cora, said, "Oh." He hesitated and said, "Ah, Chief, you want him in your office?"

Cora made a face. "What am I, Typhoid Mary? I know the accused, and suddenly you're all self-conscious around me? It's not like you're spilling state secrets here. I assume this guy's a friend of Fred Winkler, on the same crew, staying in the same motel. I'm sure he's seen Melvin acting in a manner that could be construed as hostile. There's no reason to think he killed him. Unless you're Henry Firth, who thinks everything is a reason he might have killed him. So if you want to pretend this guy's not a witness against Melvin, feel free. But it's a hollow sham, and you're not fooling anyone. What's your name?"

"Jason Tripp."

"Hi, Jason. I'm Cora Felton. And contrary to whatever impression you might get from the way Dan Finley's acting, I am not here to confuse you, cajole you, browbeat you, entice you, or in any way influence you to alter whatever account you might be inclined to give."

The young man looked overwhelmed.

"Congratulations, Cora. You've totally disrupted everything while pretending not to."

"Am I as clever as all that? Thanks, Chief, I had no idea."

"Hey, I don't know what's going on here,"

Jason said, "but I saw what I saw. You want me to tell it or not?"

"In my office," Chief Harper said.

"Spoilsport," Cora said.

Chief Harper ushered the young man into his office. He left Dan Finley outside. "See we're not disturbed."

"Gee, Dan," Cora said, "I thought we were friends."

"Come on, Cora," Dan said. "You know you lose your mind when Melvin's involved."

"I do *not* lose my mind when Melvin's involved."

"Okay, you *don't* lose your mind when Melvin's involved. But the impression you give that you *could* lose your mind when Melvin's involved is enough to make people uneasy. If I feed you a prosecution witness for lunch, I'll never hear the end of it."

"What's wrong with the witness?"

"Why do you say that?"

"If there wasn't something wrong with him, you wouldn't care."

"I care about all witnesses."

"Yeah, but with this one you're protective. You take umbrage."

"Umbrage?" Dan grinned. "You don't have to tell people you're the Puzzle Lady."

"Dan —"

175

"The guy's talking to Chief Harper. As it should be. When the chief hears what he has to say, if he wants to share it with you, no harm done. But I won't be in trouble."

"Dan, I'm sure this is a routine witness. The only thing special is the buildup. The payoff is going to be like Geraldo and Al Capone's safe. Are you old enough to know about that?"

Dan rolled his eyes. "Please."

Chief Harper came out of his office with the young man. "All right, Jason. Keep in touch. I've got your number. Don't leave town. You're going to have to talk to the county prosecutor, so keep yourself available."

"And I don't have to talk to her?"

"Not unless you want to."

"It doesn't seem like a good idea. You want to give me a ride back to work?"

"Sure thing."

Dan and Jason went out.

"Do I have to ask?" Cora said.

"It's probably better than if I volunteered it."

"Don't tell me. He not only saw Melvin hit Fred Winkler, he heard Melvin say if you come near me again, I'll kill you."

"He said that?"

"I have no idea what Melvin said. It was

something like that, wasn't it?"

"No."

"So what did he see?"

"He saw Melvin come out of the motel, go to his car, open the passenger side door, and stick a bloody knife in the glove compartment."

CHAPTER 35

"Are you an idiot?"

"Hey," Melvin said to Becky. "Is she allowed to talk to me like that?"

"I like it. That way *I* don't have to talk to you like that. What were you thinking? Stashing the murder weapon in broad daylight. Letting yourself be seen doing it."

"Wait a minute," Melvin said. "Are you going to take that guy's word over mine? And you're not even taking his word. You're taking *her* word for his word. It's unsubstantiated third-party hearsay from an unreliable source."

"You're calling me unreliable?"

"I was married to you."

"Not anymore."

"I said 'was.' Look, some friend of the dead guy wants to smear me. He shows up at the police station and says he saw me put the knife in my car. That means he was there, in the motel parking lot, when the knife was planted. Granted, *someone* put the knife in my glove compartment, and it probably was then. Now, who was it more likely to be? Me, or a friend of the victim who'd like to see me take the fall? I'm no detective, but I'd sure as hell look closely at the statement of someone who just conveniently happened to be there. Doesn't that sound fishy as hell?"

Cora frowned.

"See?" Melvin said. "Even you have doubts. And you're the one accusing me. Don't you smell a rat? You say this guy lives in my motel. Give me his name. Let's see if his story holds up to enhanced interrogation."

"Melvin, you stay away from the guy."

"How can I stay away from the guy if he's coming after me?"

"You avoid him," Becky said. "You avoid him like the plague. You see him coming, you walk the other way. Your theory sounds logical. As long as you keep away from the guy, your theory will continue to sound logical. The minute you mash his head in, no one's going to look at what you say impartially anymore. I might as well hand the prosecution a conviction on a silver platter."

"How can I let it go?"

"No one's letting it go. You want to hire

179

me to run your defense, you let me run your defense. That means giving you the best possible chance to beat the rap."

"Beat the rap? Did I really hire a lawyer who says things like 'beat the rap'?"

"I don't know why you inspire the thought," Becky said dryly.

"So this guy saw me put the knife in the car. He must be the one who phoned in the tip."

"He says he isn't."

"He *says* he isn't? We know he lied about seeing me. Now he says he isn't the one who made the call?"

"Chief Harper says he denied it."

"And that didn't make the chief skeptical?"

"Well, he told me about it. That must mean he has doubts."

"Or it could mean he doesn't," Becky said. "You're reading too much into this. The fact is *we* have doubts, whether they're based on Chief Harper's opinion, or whether he shares our opinion, or whether none of this means anything and the guy simply didn't make the call. We don't know. But the way to find out is not for you to beat it out of him. You got that?"

Melvin put up his hands. "Hey, you don't have to beat it out of me. Just as long as you're open to the suggestion and willing to act on it."

"She's willing to act on it, Melvin, if this ever comes to trial. We're trying to see that it doesn't. So this quote witness unquote is very good news. Because we don't have a lot of leads, and here's one throwing himself in our path just as pretty as you please. This guy knew you had run-ins with the decedent and he's looking for someone to frame. At the very least he's reasonable doubt. That's all well and good. But I for one don't think you killed the guy, and I'm not looking for reasonable doubt, I'm looking for proof. So you make damn sure I don't trip all over myself doing it."

"You think I'm innocent? That's really sweet."

Cora said something that not only could hardly be considered sweet but tended to indicate that the gentleman in question was a life-form barely evolved from the paramecium.

CHAPTER 36

Cora had steered clear of construction sites ever since she reached the age when workmen stopped whistling at her. She tried not to think about how long ago that was.

Jason Tripp was climbing around on a third-story scaffolding. It occurred to her how inappropriate his name was. At the moment he was walking on a plank not much wider than the plank he was carrying, a rather precarious position for a potential murder witness.

Cora didn't know when the shift ended and didn't want to call attention to herself by asking. On the other hand, she was just a stone's throw from the mall, with its friendly neighborhood Starbucks.

Cora waylaid one of the workmen on his way to the Porta-Potty. "Hey, when's your shift over?"

The look he gave her was priceless. He was clearly one of the workers from out of town, had no idea who Cora was, and thought she was hitting on him. That had to be a bit of a shock. The guy was barely old enough to vote. "Five thirty," he said, and hurried on his way.

Cora hopped in her car, sped to Starbucks, and bought herself a venti Caramel Frappuccino. So what if one of her ex-husbands had been arrested for murder and was writing a tell-all about their life together that would probably end her career, she had a scrumptious frozen plastic glass of heaven. She drove back to the construction site and sat in her car, risking brain freeze until the shift was over.

Cora was afraid Jason Tripp would go out with his pals, the guy she'd asked when the shift ended would turn out to be one of them, and she'd have to avoid being spotted by either of them. But lo and behold, at five twenty-five a familiar-looking truck pulled into the lot and Peggy Dawson got out. Now there were three people she had to keep away from. She'd be lucky if Johnny didn't show up and join the party. Or, worse, Melvin.

Neither happened. The shift ended and Peggy Dawson came flying across the lot and threw her arms around Jason Tripp's neck. He hoisted her up and spun her around, which sort of emphasized how young she actually was. Cora wondered if he knew. Or cared. Whatever the case, the way she plastered herself against him and laid a big wet one on him indicated they were more than friends.

After a minute they climbed into the truck and took off, Peggy driving.

Cora hunkered down in her Toyota Camry and made sure they didn't see her. After a minute she pulled out and followed.

Peggy drove straight to the motel. They went into unit eleven.

Cora was horribly conflicted. This was a potential jackpot, but not the one she wanted. Busting a prosecution witness for statutory rape might seem like a desperate ploy.

Cora wondered if there was anything significant about the fact it was the unit next to Melvin's. Coincidence? Probably, but interesting nonetheless. Cora pulled into a space two units down. She hoped Peggy's truck would block the motel manager's view of her car.

Cora got out and made her way down the row.

Melvin's window was still broken. Either he hadn't noticed, or the motel hadn't repaired it.

So what could she do now? She couldn't smash Jason's window, not with them in there, and she couldn't wheedle the motel manager out of *another* key.

She was in luck. The curtain was open a crack. Not that she wanted to see them going at it, but if they were, she needed to know.

She eased up close, peered through the window.

As she expected, the two of them were on the bed. However, they were not having sex, or even making out, or whatever kids called it these days.

Jason had a glass pipe in one hand and a butane torch in the other. He was sucking on the pipe while heating the bowl with the torch.

Cora had been in and out of drugs too long ago to have ever smoked crack, but that was clearly what the two of them were doing. She wondered if that was instead of underage sex, or merely a prelude to it.

Whatever the case, it looked like they'd be at it for a while. If they ever left, Cora intended to search the room. But she didn't intend to stand at the window until they did. The smart thing would be to get in her car, drive out of the lot, and watch the motel from down the street.

On the other hand, Peggy's truck was right there. Cora wondered if she'd locked it.

She hadn't.

Cora opened the passenger door and tried the glove compartment. She wasn't sure what she was looking for. A bloody knife might be nice, but that seemed too much to hope for. Though, in this case, bloody knives seemed to pop up every time she turned around.

Not this time, though. Just a handful of papers. On inspection they proved to be the truck registration, insurance card, bill of sale, a couple of old road maps, and receipts for such things as a tune-up, a lube job, a windshield wiper, and a six-pack of beer. According to the registration, her brother Johnny owned the truck. Peggy seemed to be the one who drove it most of the time, but there were no personal items of hers.

It occurred to Cora that a knife didn't have to be in the glove compartment just because the one planted in Melvin's car was. She searched under the seat, came out with a handful of dirt. A further search found nothing more significant than that.

Cora closed the door and went around to the driver's side. She hated to do it, because it exposed her to view from the manager's office. She opened the door, reached in, groped under the seat. Encountered something hard. She pulled it out, aware of the fact she was leaving fingerprints on it.

It was a plastic windshield scraper that must have been there since the last winter. She groped further, found a quarter. Probably all the money she'd ever make on this case.

Cora shoved the scraper back under the seat and checked the dashboard. The truck had nearly a hundred thousand miles on it. She wondered what year it was. It would have been on the registration, but she hadn't noticed. Was she getting careless, or just ignoring the irrelevant?

The answer was obvious. There was no way to know what was or wasn't relevant; one simply took the details in.

Cora snorted angrily, looked around the cab of the truck. She was about to slam the door when she noticed a pocket in the side, right below the crank that wound the window up and down. More than likely it held maps, only the maps had been in the glove compartment. But that didn't mean there weren't more maps.

What was she thinking? This wasn't debatable. No one was going to judge her on the advisability of searching the pocket in the door. She just had to do it. These were things that were automatic, required no thought whatsoever. And then Melvin gets in her head and suddenly nothing is automatic and everything requires thought. And then she's standing there like a dummy when Peggy comes storming out and wants to know what she's doing in her truck. Assuming the police hadn't already showed up to demand the same answer.

Cora reached in the pocket in the door and encountered a folded paper. Most likely a map, and probably the one she used most, since it was the only thing in the pocket.

It wasn't a map. There was nothing printed on it. It was just a sheet of white paper.

Cora unfolded it.

It was a crossword puzzle.

Across

1 Prime number
5 Coffee, slangily
9 Basilica recesses
14 Has _____ (is connected)
15 Lena of "Havana"
16 Shannon Airport's county
17 Start of a message
19 Shire of "Rocky" movies
20 Relax, as rules
21 Midpoint

22 Chucklehead
24 Manufactured
25 Baseball card tidbits
29 More of the message
34 Spring up
35 "Dream Lover" singer Bobby
36 "_____ Believer" (Monkees hit)
37 Spanish Surrealist Joan
38 Ira who wrote "Rosemary's Baby"

39 Cattle rancher's tool
40 Nectar collector
41 Pal of Theodore and Alvin
42 Michelangelo masterpiece
43 More of the message
45 Rear-_____ (road mishap)
46 Oak Ridge's state: Abbr.
47 Heeded a "Down in front!" cry
49 Slackens off
52 Mortar mate
57 Hybrid big cat
58 End of the message
61 _____firma
62 Sign of decay
63 Affleck thriller set in Iran
64 Preferred invitees
65 Borscht vegetable
66 Reacts to a bad call

Down
1 Go down the tubes
2 Help desk offering, briefly
3 "In _____veritas"
4 Mireille of "The Catch"
5 _____Hopkins University
6 Pugilism's self-proclaimed "great-est"
7 Auto registration fig.
8 "Hulk" director Lee
9 Followed, as advice

10 Eris is a dwarf one
11 Margarita garnish
12 HOMES member
13 Affix a brand to
18 Kid around with
21 Log dwelling
23 Backup band member
24 Quantico group
25 Brazilian dance
26 Took a shot at
27 Ran on TV
28 General _____'s chicken
30 Enjoy to the utmost
31 Brought onboard
32 Overdo it onstage
33 Control tower device
38 Creditors' claims
39 Fraternity jewelry
41 Make a mockery of
42 Pianist Nero
44 Web-footed mammals
48 In pieces
49 Utah ski spot
50 Jessica of "Total Recall"
51 Prefix with culture
53 Grab with a toothpick
54 "Comin' _____the Rye"
55 Toy brick brand
56 Bow-toting deity
58 Amorphous mass

59 "To a" work
60 One of "them"

CHAPTER 37

"Tell me I'm not crazy."

"You're not crazy. Anything else?"

Cora glared at her niece. "You're not helping."

"I'm very agreeable. What's the matter?"

"Peggy's got another puzzle."

"And she wants you to solve it?"

"She doesn't know I have it."

"Then what's the problem?"

"This is why you're not helping. Stop asking complicated questions."

"What's so complicated?"

"Like that one. See, this is why you're not helping."

Sherry turned back to the computer. She was in the middle of composing the next Puzzle Lady column, and she didn't want to be interrupted. The chance of Cora understanding that defied the laws of probability.

"Come on, help me out. Peggy Dawson

has a puzzle. She has no right to have a puzzle. She can't *do* puzzles. She comes to *me* when she has a puzzle. A mistake, but one most people make."

"What's your point?"

"Why does she have a puzzle? One was sent to her anonymously, that's what started this whole fiasco. There's no way on earth she should have a puzzle."

"Couldn't the person who sent her one send her another?"

"I can't think why, but never mind that. Say she had one. She'd immediately want to know what the puzzle said. She was all excited with her theories about how the first puzzle had to do with the murder. She gets another puzzle, she's going to think the same thing."

"Oh, for goodness' sakes."

"Doesn't that make sense?"

Sherry sighed, swiveled her desk chair away from the keyboard. "You wanna come down to earth and tell me what this is all about?"

Cora told Sherry about following Peggy and Jason to the motel and searching the truck.

Sherry's interest picked up. "They were doing drugs?"

"Don't get sidetracked. The point is the

194

puzzle."

"Aren't drugs often a motive for crime?"

"Absolutely. I'll keep it in mind. Get back to the puzzle."

"Fine." Sherry swung around and started typing in "Crossword Compiler."

"Not that puzzle!" Cora said. "Damn it, you're doing that deliberately."

"No fun, is it? You know how often you do that to me?"

"No. Enlighten me," Cora said sarcastically. "This isn't funny, Sherry. Melvin's done something really, really bad. I don't know what it is, but it isn't murder. Well, I *do* know what it is. He's written this damn book, and I've got to do something about that, but getting arrested for murder has sort of pushed it onto the back burner. I've got to get him off the hook so I can get him back *on* the hook so I can apply some pressure and keep him from ruining both our lives. Is that important enough for you to take time off from your stupid Puzzle Lady column and help me out?"

"I was trying to, before you got distracted by drugs."

"*I* didn't get distracted by drugs. *You* got distracted by drugs. I mentioned them as part of the explanation you demanded before you were even willing to talk to me,

195

and you went off on a tangent."

"Talk about going off on a tangent."

"I'm *not* going off on a tangent. I'm trying to get back to the crossword puzzle. Come on, you know me, Sherry. I'm focused on the crossword puzzle, and nothing is going to distract me until we deal with that."

"You have my full attention." Sherry spun around, folded her hands, presented a picture of complete contrition.

Cora paused for breath. She opened her mouth and suddenly frowned. "Where's Jennifer?"

"Playing with Ricky."

"Who's Ricky?"

"A boy from school."

"She's out on a *date*?"

"A playdate."

"I'll bet it is."

"They're children."

"So was I, and I knew the difference between boys and girls."

"I'm proud of you. You want me to call Ricky's mother and ask her if they're playing doctor?"

"Make fun of me all you like. Ricky may seem cute now, but the next thing you know he's in jail writing a tell-all."

Sherry put up her hands. "Fine. I'm giving Peggy's puzzle all the due consideration it deserves. Can I see it?"

"Thought you'd never ask." Cora pulled the puzzle out of her drawstring purse and handed it over.

Sherry unfolded it and took a look. "Well, it's not a copy of the puzzle you already gave me."

"Don't you think I'd have mentioned that?"

"Sure, if you noticed."

"I'd have noticed."

"I can only go by my experience."

"I learn from experience. I looked at the puzzle."

Sherry picked up a pencil and tore into the puzzle.

"It takes so little time for you to do it and then you crab about it."

"Shhh."

"You spend more time arguing with me than you do solving the puzzle. And I can't even distract you when you're working. You tell me to shut up, and your pencil never stops moving."

"I swear, I'm going to brain you with it."

"Oh, hit me over the head with a cross-word puzzle. That must really hurt."

"It will if I hit you with the puzzle on the computer. Here. Done. The crime is solved and we can go back to real life."

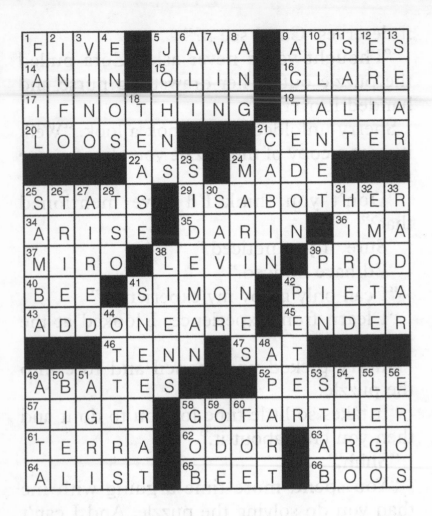

Cora snatched the puzzle.

"IF NOTHING
IS A BOTHER
ADD ONE ARE
GO FARTHER."

She looked up. "That makes no sense."
"What a surprise," Sherry said.

198

"No, it really makes no sense. I'm not saying in terms of murders or whatever, I'm just saying. It's total nonsense."

"I think you've described your whole career."

"Damn it, Sherry. You make up these things. Is there any point to this one?"

"Not at first glance."

"Well, glance again. After all I went through to get the damn thing, I'd like to know what it means."

"All you went through? You searched one truck."

"Sherry."

"If the puzzle's meaningless, that's not my fault. I can stare at it all day, it's going to say the same thing. As to what it means, that's your department. Related to the crime, related to itself, related to reality. I can tell you this: In and of itself, it means absolutely nothing."

"So why does Peggy Dawson have a meaningless crossword puzzle folded up in the door of her truck?"

"I don't know, but as you pointed out, don't you have more important things to deal with?"

"Not at the moment."

"How about following the guy Peggy's with to find out what he's up to."

"Turns out it's drugs and teenage girls. Which is a real kick in the teeth."

"Why?"

"Guy claims he saw Melvin come out of his motel room and put the knife in his car. If the guy's working construction at the mall, what the hell's he doing at the motel on his lunch break? You bring your lunch or go to a fast-food place at the mall. Turns out his story might hold up. Guy's smoking crack, with a pipe and a torch, and all that. It's not the same thing as smoking a joint, he's gotta go back to the room to do it."

"He's gonna claim *that* in court?"

"Never mind court. I'm talking plausibility. I hear his story, I dismiss it as crap. The more you ground it in reality, the more it sounds true. I'm not talking about a jury. I'm talking about me."

"You're worried for Melvin."

"Oh, stop it. Everyone acts like there's something between me and Melvin. The last thing between us was a restraining order. Damn it, Sherry, I don't really feel like being kidded."

"Hadn't noticed."

CHAPTER 38

"The prosecution's key witness is a crack-head."

"Huh?" Becky said.

"He gets high on crack and puts the move on teenage girls."

"Are you serious?"

"Yeah. It's good news and bad news. The good news is he's an unreliable witness. The bad news is he smokes crack so he had a reason to be at the motel when he said he was."

Becky tossed off her scotch and signaled the bartender. "I'll have another. Better make it a double."

"Getting drunk won't help."

"Couldn't hurt."

"As a card-carrying alcoholic, I beg to differ. Where's Melvin? I thought he'd be hitting on you."

"I guess he has other fish to fry."

"That's not good."

"Why not?"

"It just isn't. You don't need Melvin getting into more trouble."

"You think he's out with another woman?"

"That's not what I was saying at all. Jesus. You and Sherry."

"What?"

"I don't have a thing for Melvin. Besides animosity and dread."

"The start of any good relationship."

"Becky."

"So where do you think he is?"

"Alone sipping tea and reading the Bible. Why? I don't care where he is as long as he stays out of trouble."

"You should really keep tabs on him, get him to take you out to dinner."

Cora suggested something Becky might have for dinner not apt to be featured on any restaurant menu.

"Nice talk." Becky sipped her scotch.

"I didn't tell you what I got."

"What did you get?"

Cora handed over the puzzle.

Becky unfolded it. "What's this?" She read the theme answer. "This makes no sense."

"Thank you. It's good to have one's opinion validated."

"You stole this from the cab of Peggy Dawson's truck?"

"Actually from the cab of Johnny Dawson's truck, according to the registration."

"Is that right?"

"Yeah, and this is the most helpful clue I could come up with. The puzzle makes no sense. In itself, and in the fact she had it. Why would Peggy Dawson have a puzzle? She had one puzzle, and she gave it to me. Triumphantly, thinking it solved the crime. She gets another puzzle, and she couldn't care less."

"She must have got it awhile ago, before any of this happened."

"Then why didn't she want to know what that puzzle said? And how did she get it?"

"Maybe she didn't get it. Maybe it was just folded up and stuck in the truck."

"By whom?"

"Her brother. Didn't you say it's his truck?"

"His name's on the registration. He doesn't use it."

"Uh huh."

"Wanna drive out to the motel?"

"Why?"

"He's your client. There's nothing wrong with you driving out there."

"He's not there."

"You don't know that. He might very well be there. And we could see if Peggy's truck was still there."

"You think it is?"

"I don't know. I never smoked crack. I don't know how long it takes."

"They might be doing something else. I believe you have experience in *that* department."

Cora's suggestions for what Becky might conceivably eat was rapidly evolving into a three-course meal.

CHAPTER 39

Cora stopped at the side of the road in sight of the motel. Peggy's truck was gone.

"Looks like we're too late," Becky said.

"Yeah. Wanna see a crack pipe?"

"We are *not* breaking into that motel room."

"Are you sure?"

"Yes, I'm sure. I'm an attorney at law. Do you know what it would look like if I were caught breaking and entering the room of a prosecution witness?"

Cora shrugged. "You photograph well."

"I'm not doing it, Cora, and neither are you. There's nothing to gain and everything to lose."

"How do you figure that?"

"Just the fact we're doing it gives his story credibility. It's probably the only thing that does. I can tie him in knots on why he went back to the motel. I can get him on the defensive and make it look like he's lying.

It's a little easier to do if I haven't been arrested for breaking into his room."

"So don't get caught."

"I'm not going to get caught. I'm going to stay in the car, go back to town, and thank my lucky stars I was born with the sense not to do it."

"That's only because you don't see an upside. If he had something you wanted, you'd be singing a different tune."

"So would you. You'd be gung-ho to find that such and such that proves dear Melvin was pure as the driven snow."

"And what the hell is that all about?" Cora said. "Who drives snow?"

"You're the wordsmith. You tell me. But tell me while we're driving."

Cora started the car and pulled out.

She turned into the motel.

"What are you doing?"

"Turning around. You said you wanted to go back to town, didn't you? Or did you want me to drive to New York?"

"Fine, turn around."

"You got it."

Cora drove down the row and parked in front of Melvin's unit.

"What are you doing?" Becky demanded.

"Solving your problem."

"*You're* my problem. I want to go back to town."

"No, you don't. You just don't want to get arrested breaking into Jason's room. You're not doing that. You're calling on Melvin. Melvin's not a prosecution witness. He's your client. You've got every right to call on him."

"Melvin's not there."

"Well, if you're going to quibble."

"I'm not breaking into Melvin's room, either."

"Relax. We're not breaking and entering."

"We're not?"

"Absolutely not. Look. The window is already broken. In the interest of your client, it's your duty as an attorney to make sure nothing is stolen."

"No, it isn't."

"So think of something better. You're the lawyer." Cora reached in the broken window pane and unlocked the door. "Hey, look. It's open."

"Damn it, Cora —"

But Cora was already inside. Becky stood there for a moment in helpless frustration. A car pulled up to another unit and four young men in jeans and T-shirts got out, obviously workers from the construction site. At least Jason wasn't among them. Still,

Becky didn't want to be caught standing there. Cursing Cora, she stepped inside.

"Wise decision," Cora said.

"Strangling you would be a wise decision. Following you into a motel room is like playing Russian roulette."

"Before you pull the trigger, you want to close the door?"

Becky glared at Cora and slammed it shut.

"You're obviously new to confidential investigations, but, just as a hint, most private eyes favor not calling attention to themselves when attempting illegal entry."

"Fine. I'll be quiet as a mouse. You mind telling me what you're looking for?"

"An explanation for what's going on. We've got a case that doesn't make sense. I'd be happy for the slightest hint."

"You think you'll find it here?"

"I don't know. But I've learned from bitter experience that taking Melvin at his word isn't a great idea. The man has many faults, but at least he's predictable. He has one other virtue."

"What's that?"

"He's not the type of guy to run around with a briefcase. Unless he's carrying it as a prop when he's pretending to work."

"You liked him once."

"Liked doesn't quite describe it."

208

"What does?"

"I had a drinking problem."

Cora flopped Melvin's briefcase on the bed, snapped it open, and pulled out a pile of brochures.

"What's that?" Becky said.

"Real estate listings."

"So he really is working."

"Selling property he doesn't own is one of his specialties. He used to sell land in Florida."

"That he didn't own?"

"Of course not. It was a good gig while it lasted."

"What happened?"

"People tried to take possession. It was all right as long as the houses were vacant. Unfortunately, he sold the same one to two people. They showed up at the same time."

Cora riffled through the papers.

"Anything interesting?" Becky said.

"No file marked *Bimbos*. Maybe he's slowing down."

"They're probably on his iPhone."

Cora pulled out a folder marked *Sales*. It was bulging.

"He sold all that?" Becky said.

"I doubt it."

Cora flipped it open. On the top were what appeared to be a couple of sales contracts. The rest consisted of bills, receipts, flyers, letters, and advertisements. There was even the occasional girlie pic.

"Once again Melvin does not disappoint," Cora said. "What you see is not what you get." She slipped the folder back in the briefcase, pulled out another. The folder marked *Rentals* was similar. So were the ones marked *Pending* and *Closing*.

"Ah, here it is," Cora said.

"What's that?"

"Melvin's contract with the publisher."

"Oh?"

"Here. Take a look."

"Why?"

"I thought you could look it over."

"What for?"

"A flaw, a loophole, an exception. Whatever the hell you lawyers call it when you don't want something to be legally binding."

"A publishing contract is legally binding."

"Let's not be hasty. This isn't a work of fiction. Though, in Melvin's case, it might as well be. He's going to be stating things as fact. About me. Hell, it's right in the title. Doesn't that make a difference?"

"No."

Cora made a face. "You're a lawyer. You're supposed to take your client's position."

"Oh, you're my client?"

"In the copyright infringement suit."

"What copyright infringement suit?"

"Are you kidding? I'm the Puzzle Lady. And he's writing about me. If anybody's gonna write about me it should be me."

"You think all biographies are autobiographies?"

"Just read it, will you? While I give the room a once-over."

Cora searched the room. She didn't expect to find anything, Melvin hadn't done it, the killer had planted the knife in his car. The killer wouldn't have planted anything in his motel room. It was risky, and there was no need. Nonetheless, Cora made a show of searching the dresser. As she pulled the drawers open, she spied over her shoulder to make sure Becky was reading the contract. Becky was. Cora breathed a sigh of relief. If there was any way to stop Melvin from publishing the book, Becky would find it.

Cora pulled the bottom drawer open and her face froze.

Wadded up in a corner of the drawer was a bloody handkerchief. At least it appeared to be blood. It might have been some other red stain, but Cora didn't think so.

Her head was whirling. She'd just gotten

through convincing herself the killer wouldn't have left anything in Melvin's motel room, and now this.

Cora glanced over her shoulder again. Becky was still reading the contract.

Cora palmed the handkerchief and stuffed it deep into the bottom of her drawstring purse.

She closed the bottom drawer, stood up, and turned around.

Becky looked up from the contract. "Okay, I read it."

Cora almost asked her what. She recovered in time to say, "And?" She said it as casually as possible, then panicked, realizing the contract was important and she wouldn't be casual about it.

"You're screwed."

Cora exhaled. "Come on, Becky, what am I paying you for?"

"You're not paying me."

"Well, if you're going to be a stickler about it. Wouldn't it be a contingency fee, anyway?"

"Do you want to stop publication or collect damages for it?"

"Whatever works. Give me the contract."

Cora took the contract, jammed it back in the briefcase. It caught on a file folder, one she hadn't seen before. She pulled it out, stuck the contract in. The folder appeared to be empty. It was flat and unmarked. Cora flipped it open.

Inside was a single slip of paper. She picked it up and her mouth fell open. "Uh oh!"

"What?"

"Let's get the hell out of here!"

Cora slammed the briefcase shut, stuck it on the floor where she'd found it. She grabbed the manila folder and hightailed it out the door.

Becky caught up just as Cora was starting the car. Becky jumped in, and Cora took off.

"What are you running away from?" Becky said.

"I'm not running away."

"What are you doing?"

"I'm suppressing evidence."

"What evidence?"

"That." Cora jerked her thumb at the folder.

Peggy picked it up. "What's this?"

"It's a receipt for something Melvin bought at Target."

"What?"

"A hunting knife."

CHAPTER 40

A couple of miles down the road, Cora slowed the car.

"There. No one's following us. Let's take the bypass nice and easy and come in from the other side of town."

Becky's world had collapsed. "Melvin's guilty."

"Not necessarily."

"He had the murder weapon. It wasn't planted on him. He bought it."

"The receipt could have been planted on him."

"You think it was?"

"No."

"So you think he's guilty."

"Buying the knife looks bad."

"Ya think?"

Cora shook her head. "Not the way you mean."

"It means he did it."

"Not necessarily."

"Come on. He bought the murder weapon."

"It's worse than that."

"How can it be worse than that?"

"Did you see the date on the receipt?"

"What about it?"

"It's today."

Becky blinked. "Are you kidding me?"

"No."

"How does that make any sense?"

"The cops find a knife in his car. Melvin says oops and rushes out to Target and buys a knife so he can claim it's the knife the police found. He keeps the sales receipt so he can prove the knife was bought *after* the murder."

"The knife the police found isn't the knife Melvin bought?"

"Of course not."

"So where's the knife Melvin bought?"

"At the bottom of the deepest lake. One thing's for sure, it won't turn up. And if they try him for murder, Melvin's gonna hand you that receipt and insist you introduce it into evidence and argue the knife the police found in his glove compartment is the knife he bought at Target after the crime."

"But he bought it *after* the police found the knife in his car," Becky protested.

Cora shook her head. "The sales slip is

dated, but it doesn't have the *time* of purchase on it. He bought it the same day. He'll expect you to argue that he bought it *before* the knife was found in his car, and not after."

"For which I could be disbarred," Becky said.

"Nonsense. Lawyers argue things that aren't true all the time."

"Sure. They make them up. Which is perfectly within the law. It's what lawyers do. Present a reasonable hypothesis other than guilt. What they don't do is blatantly lie. They do not present false evidence and claim things they know for a fact are untrue."

"Sure they do," Cora said.

"I know they do. And if they're caught, they can be disbarred. For suborning perjury and giving false evidence."

"Relax. I just saved you from all that. I got the receipt. You won't have to present it because Melvin doesn't have it."

"So I'm only guilty of suppressing evidence. Who could object to that?"

"You're not suppressing evidence. I am."

"I'm an accessory before and after the fact."

"I beg to differ. Did you look closely at the receipt?"

"No."

"Well don't look now. You don't know what it is. You only know what I told you. That's hearsay. For all you know it's a recipe for cheesecake. I wouldn't give it a moment's thought."

Cora had looped all around and was coming into town. They passed the Country Kitchen.

"Oh, look, there's Peggy's truck."

"Ah," Becky said. "Another place you made an illegal search. You plan on visiting them all?"

"No, but that's a great idea."

"What?"

"How about we combine the two?"

"What are you talking about?"

"Put Melvin's receipt in Peggy's truck."

"I'll wring your neck."

"Relax, I'm not going to do it. I've got plans for that receipt."

"Like what?"

"Like hold it over your head whenever I want to put pressure on you."

"I'm not in the mood, Cora."

"I know. I'll drop you off in town."

Cora drove into town and pulled up in front of the police station.

Becky got out but didn't close the door. She leaned into the car, looked at Cora suspiciously. "You're not going back to the Country Kitchen."

"Why would I do that?"

"To put the receipt in Peggy's truck."

"I won't."

"If I find out you did . . ."

"How would you find out?"

"You're going to do it?"

"I'm *not* going to do it."

"Swear to God?"

"Absolutely. If a receipt is found in Peggy's truck, it will be because she bought the identical knife."

"Cora."

"She didn't, I won't, it's not happening. Worry about something else. You got a lot of choices. Pick one."

Becky heaved a huge sigh and slammed the door.

Cora turned the car around and drove out of town at a leisurely pace. Becky watched her all the way.

As soon as she was out of sight, Cora sped up and raced to the Country Kitchen. She pulled into a spot near Peggy's truck, put the car in Park but left the motor running.

Cora hadn't lied to Becky. She had no intention of putting the receipt in Peggy's truck. She had something better.

Cora grabbed her drawstring purse, hurried to Peggy's truck, and wrenched the driver's-side door open. The overhead light came on, but there was nothing she could do about that. She leaned in, rummaged through her purse, and pulled out the bloody handkerchief. She unfolded it and spread it out on the seat of the truck.

Before she closed the door, she looked closely to make sure it was really blood. She'd feel like a damn fool if turned out to be one Melvin had used to wipe off lipstick.

It was blood, all right. Lipstick didn't coagulate. At least as far as she knew. Was curdle the same as coagulate? As a wordsmith she should know that.

Her face froze.

Cora couldn't plant the handkerchief in Peggy's Dawson's truck. She couldn't plant it anywhere at all.

She snatched it up again, stuck it back in her purse.

Cora slammed the door of the truck, ran back to her car, and flew out of the parking lot.

CHAPTER 41

Cora skidded up the driveway, spinning her wheels and scattering gravel in all directions. She lurched to a stop, grabbed her purse, and hopped out of the car.

Sherry's car was gone. So was her husband Aaron's. This time of day the young reporter would be in his office at the *Bakerhaven Gazette*. There was no one home.

Cora ran up the walk, flung open the door. Buddy scooted out. She left him to his own devices, went inside, and dumped her drawstring purse out on the kitchen table. She grabbed the bloody handkerchief and sat down to give it a closer look.

It was one of Melvin's old handkerchiefs, dating back to the days they were together. Melvin had given her one every now and then when his escapades had reduced her to tears. It wasn't often she let him see her that way. On the other hand, tears were a useful weapon for a woman, and Cora wasn't above using them. On such occasions, he always had a handkerchief. This was one of them. It had the same old laundry mark.

Cora sucked in her breath. The handkerchief hadn't been planted on Melvin. The handkerchief was Melvin's.

Melvin was the killer.

Buddy scratching at the screen door brought Cora back to reality. She let him in, and he raced around the kitchen, yipping and demanding food. It was purely a ritual. He *had* food, he had just chosen not to eat it because no one was home.

Cora usually ignored him. Today, she wanted him to shut up. She jerked the refrigerator door open, grabbed a piece of bologna, tore it up, and dropped it in his bowl. Buddy thought he'd died and gone to heaven.

Cora went out to the back porch and took the lid off the garbage can for recyclables. She pawed through and found a plastic takeout container from the Chinese restaurant. It was a large one, had probably held orange beef or sesame chicken. She found the plastic lid, took them to the sink, and gave them a good wash. They'd already been rinsed out, but she did it again. It was the first time she'd ever washed a recyclable item, but the novelty was lost on her. She worked feverishly, rubbing the container bone dry with a dish towel.

She put the bloody handkerchief inside, snapped on the top.

Cora grabbed a flashlight, took the container, and went out the kitchen door, with Buddy in hot pursuit.

She found a shovel in the toolshed and headed for the trees out back.

Between the oaks and maples was a small stand of pine. Dead needles formed a carpet underneath. Cora pushed them aside, got down to the dirt. She grabbed the shovel and attacked it. It was laced with roots from the trees, not easy digging. She chopped them away with the blade of the shovel, dug a shallow hole. She put the plastic takeout container in, covered it with dirt, and pushed dead needles over the top.

Buddy watched the whole process. He didn't bark. The dog that didn't bark in the night.

Cora giggled. She was getting giddy. Compounding felonies would do that to a person.

Cora stood up and inspected her work with the flashlight. She couldn't tell. By the light of day it might be a different matter. But in a few days it would be fine.

Cora came back around the house just as Sherry was parking the car.

Jennifer exploded from the front seat crying, "Auntie Cora! Auntie Cora!"

Buddy intercepted her and they took off over the lawn.

"What were you doing out back?" Sherry said.

"Nothing."

"What do you mean, nothing? You're acting like a giddy schoolgirl." Sherry's eyes widened. "Were you smoking?"

"No."

"It's understandable. You've been under a lot of stress."

"Wanna smell my breath?"

"I've had more attractive offers."

"I wish I had."

Jennifer and Buddy came running back. Cora seized the opportunity to change the subject.

"How was her date?"

"Great. He took her to dinner."

"It always starts with dinner."

"At McDonald's."

"Amateur. Though I had a date take me to McDonald's once."

"Did you have a Happy Meal?"

"He didn't. Where's Aaron?"

"Working late. There's been a murder, in

case you haven't heard."

"Does he have any news?"

"I don't know. Do you?"

"Nothing he can print."

"What did you do now?"

"What do you mean?"

"Come on, Cora. You're running around in the dark with a flashlight."

"What's your point?"

"You're up to something.

"I'm always up to something. That's my nature."

Headlights came up the driveway. Aaron pulled up and got out.

Jennifer screamed, "Daddy! Daddy! Daddy!" and flew across the lawn.

"You shouldn't let her run around in the dark," Cora said. "What if Aaron didn't see her?"

Daddy was already spinning his little girl in a circle. "How come she's out so late?"

"She just got home herself. She had a playdate."

"Sherry's pimping her out," Cora said. "You should have a talk with her."

"Oh?"

"The Stebbins boy," Sherry said.

"He took her to dinner," Cora said.

"Alone?"

"There might have been a grown-up in-

224

volved."

"Why are you all outside?"

"Cora was up to something in the back-yard," Sherry said.

"Please," Cora said. "Not in front of the C-H-I-L-D."

"She can spell," Sherry said.

"Then not in front of the R-E-P-O-R-T-E-R."

"What the hell is going on?"

"Daddy said 'hell.' "

"It's her fault." Aaron pointed at Cora.

"Come on," Sherry said. "Let's go inside and put someone to bed."

"Who?" Jennifer said.

"Guess."

"Auntie Cora?" Jennifer said brightly.

"Judges?" Sherry said.

"You guys are having entirely too much fun," Aaron said.

"Okay, bum us out," Cora said. "Tell us about *your* day."

Aaron looked at Sherry. "What's with her?"

"It's the Melvin effect. She's getting giddy."

They went inside. Jennifer and Buddy raced upstairs to wash up. The grown-ups went in the kitchen and Sherry made coffee.

"So, what'd you write?" Cora demanded.

Aaron looked at Sherry. "She ever let you catch your breath?"

"Yeah, I wouldn't mind hearing what you wrote, either," Sherry said.

"I wrote an exclusive interview with Melvin Crabtree."

"Really?" Cora said.

"Yeah," Aaron said. "I'd be more thrilled if everyone and his brother didn't have an exclusive interview with Melvin Crabtree. The only thing exclusive about it was he didn't say the same thing he did in his exclusive interview with Rick Reed."

"Melvin doesn't stick to a script. He has a few talking points he touches on, the rest he improvises. So what did he tell you?"

"The witness who claims he put the knife in the car isn't mistaken; he's lying. The guy's a friend of the victim with an ax to grind. He was going to say he saw *Johnny* put the knife in his car, but when the police arrested him he changed his tune."

"I like that," Cora said.

"I thought you would."

"That's not what he told Rick Reed?"

"No. He told him he has no idea why this is happening, he figures it's just locals trying to blame their troubles on an outsider."

"Was Rick happy with that statement?"

"Rick's too dumb to know it's not news. If he gets the principals on camera, he's happy."

"And that's all?"

"Relax. He didn't say anything about the book."

Cora looked at Sherry. "You *told* him?" she said accusingly.

"He's my husband."

"Melvin was my husband. I didn't tell him everything."

"How'd that work out?"

Cora glowered at Sherry and turned to Aaron. "You're not writing, alluding to, hinting at, or in any other way intimating that there is now, or might ever be, a project under way in which Melvin would be recounting anything he might know about me from our years together."

Aaron put up his hands. "Hey, my lips are sealed. If Melvin spills the beans, there's nothing I can do."

There came the sound of tires on gravel, and headlights raked the window.

"Expecting anybody?" Aaron said.

"Probably for Jennifer," Cora said, on her way to the front door. "Once a girl gets a reputation . . ."

A pickup truck stopped at the top of the drive. Peggy Dawson hopped out and ran

2			9					
3				1			5	
						8	2	4
9					1		3	
1		6						7
			8	5	4	1		
			9	4				
			7			3		8
			6			7		

up the path.

Cora's heart sank.

She was waving a piece of paper.

CHAPTER 42

Cora's fears were groundless.

"I found a Sudoku!" Peggy cried.

Cora let out her breath. She hadn't realized she was holding it. What a relief. As bad as she was with crosswords, she was good at Sudoku. She could whiz through one in minutes. Instead of having to tap-dance around the fact she couldn't do the puzzle, she would give the girl a flash of her expertise and send her on her way.

A little ritual whining was called for, however.

"Oh, for goodness' sakes," Cora said. "I am not open day and night as your personal puzzle solver. Why didn't you take this to Harvey Beerbaum?"

"I didn't know he could do Sudoku."

"He can. Not as well as I can, but he can."

"Please," Peggy pleaded. "I don't wanna go over to that guy's house after dark. He's creepy."

The idea of Harvey Beerbaum as a wicked seductor of young girls struck Cora as funny. "All right," she said magnanimously, "just this once. Come in and I'll solve your puzzle for you."

Cora brought Peggy into the kitchen and introduced her to Sherry. Aaron had gone upstairs to put Jennifer to bed.

"I was making coffee," Sherry said. "You want some?"

"Sure."

"Cream and sugar?"

"Black."

Cora suppressed a smile. Tough teenager. Drank it black to show off. Coffee was better with milk and sugar.

"What you got there?" Sherry asked.

"It's a Sudoku," Cora said. "I told her I'd do it just this once."

"That's nice of you. You've had a long day."

"It's easier than arguing. You got a pencil, Sherry? You must have one around here somewhere." Cora started jerking open drawers.

"It won't be with the silverware," Sherry said. "Try the utility drawer."

"Which one is that?"

"How many years have we lived in this house?"

"It's not enough I gotta do a damn puzzle, I have to play guessing games?"

"Next to the stove."

Cora pulled the drawer open. She found a box of kitchen matches, a church key, as she used to call it when she was drinking, a Swiss Army knife, and one gnarled, stubby pencil.

"Ah, here we go. I'll have this done in no time."

Cora sat at the kitchen table, picked up the puzzle. "Where'd you find this, Peggy?"

"Someone left it in my truck."

That gave Cora a turn. She'd been close to leaving something else in Peggy's truck. "When was that?"

"Just now. I was having a cheeseburger at the Country Kitchen. I came out and there it was."

"Someone left it there during dinner?"

"That's right."

"That's strange. You sure it wasn't there before?"

"It was right on the seat. Does that look like I sat on it?"

The paper was unwrinkled. "No, it doesn't," Cora conceded.

"See? Someone left it there during dinner. It's strange, but there you are. That's why I'm bringing it to you. Because it's strange."

2	8	5	9	4	6	1	7	3
3	7	4	2	1	8	9	5	6
6	1	9	3	5	7	8	2	4
9	4	8	7	2	1	6	3	5
1	5	6	4	3	9	2	8	7
7	2	3	6	8	5	4	1	9
8	3	7	1	9	4	5	6	2
4	6	1	5	7	2	3	9	8
5	9	2	8	6	3	7	4	1

"All right. Let's solve this sucker."

"How long's it going to take you?"

"Got a stopwatch?"

"You're that fast?"

"I am," Cora said.

She flew through the puzzle. It was only moderately hard. She was done in minutes.

Peggy was duly impressed. "Wow, that's something." She grabbed the puzzle, peered at it. "So what's it mean?"

"It doesn't mean anything."

"It has to."

"It can't. It's just a bunch of numbers."

"Yeah, but —"

"But what?"

"Someone left me a crossword. Now they left me a Sudoku. Maybe the Sudoku refers to it."

"I don't see how."

"Well, look," Peggy said. She pulled the crossword out of her hip pocket and unfolded it. "A crossword has numbers. Twenty-six across, seventeen down. Why couldn't it refer to that?"

"Smart girl," Sherry said.

Cora gave her a look that might conceivably kill. "Yes. Very smart girl. But there's a flaw in your logic. A Sudoku has eighty-one numbers, the numbers one through nine, each used nine times. There's no across, there's no down, there's no way to break the numbers up."

"Well, couldn't the crossword be referring to the Sudoku?"

"It's a fascinating theory. Feel free to pursue it."

"But you're the Puzzle Lady."

"I am. That doesn't mean I can find a relationship that doesn't exist. I will look. If anything comes to mind, I will let you know. But nothing jumps out at me."

"Okay," Peggy said. "You can keep the puzzle. I made a copy."

"That's fine. Of course I don't have a copy of the Sudoku, but you could drop one off tomorrow. Just stick it in our mailbox."

"I'll run one off now," Sherry said.

"You can do that?"

"Sure. I'll scan it and print it."

Sherry grabbed the Sudoku and headed for the office.

"Well, aren't you helpful," Cora said.

She didn't sound sincere.

CHAPTER 43

Cora banged on Melvin's door. She was going to bang on the window, but it was still broken. No reason to call attention to it.

Melvin swung the door open and smiled. "I knew you'd give in."

"I'm not giving anything, Melvin."

Cora pushed by him into the room and looked around as if seeing it for the first time. "Oh, God, how can you live like this?"

"It does need a woman's touch," Melvin said. "Then again, so do I."

"Yeah, it ain't happening. Listen, there's been some developments in the case you should know about."

"Whatever they are, they don't involve me."

"How do you know that?"

"Nothing in the case involves me."

"Peggy Dawson found a Sudoku in her truck."

"Why should I care about that?"

"Because she'd been running around with the guy who saw you put the murder weapon in your car."

"What's that got to do with a Sudoku?"

"Absolutely nothing. But Peggy's been bombarding me with puzzles, insisting they have something to do with the murder."

"Do they?"

"No, but it doesn't matter. The point is, Peggy's advancing theories. The puzzle's just a means of introduction. She's pushing an agenda."

"What agenda?"

"Her brother was arrested for the murder. Peggy didn't like that. Lo and behold, evidence shows up exonerating her brother and implicating you. And who is the witness who saw you putting the murder weapon in your car? The guy she's palling around with."

"When you put it like that, it sounds bad."

"Would you care to phrase it so it sounds good? When you go to jail, I'd like it to be for something you actually did."

"That's sweet. Too bad you quit drinking. I could offer you something."

"And we all know what."

"Why, Cora, you naughty wench."

"That's not why I came over here, Melvin."

236

"Sure it is."

"In your dreams."

Cora felt virtuous as she left the motel.
If only she didn't feel like she just had a
narrow escape.

CHAPTER 44

Cora woke up to Buddy barking hysterically and someone banging on the door. She threw on a bathrobe, stumbled through the living room, and flung the door open for Chief Harper.

"I have very bad news."

"For whom?"

"For Melvin," Harper said, and pushed his way in.

"How could things be any worse for Melvin? He's already been arrested for murder."

"I got another corpse."

Cora's face fell. "Don't tell me."

Harper nodded. "That's right. The chief witness against him was found last night in the mall parking lot with a hunting knife in his back. At least this time we don't have to play hide-and-seek with the murder weapon. It's right where it should be."

"The victim might not think so."

"Too bad Melvin's out on bail, or he'd have a rock-solid alibi for this one."

"Thank you."

"For what?"

"Assuming he didn't do it."

"I was being facetious."

"I'm surprised you know what it means."

"Hey, don't shoot the messenger. I'm sorry the news is bad."

"Have you picked Melvin up?"

"Well, that's the thing."

"You can't find him?"

"He's not at his motel."

"Where else have you looked?"

Harper looked sheepish. "Well —"

Cora's eyes widened. "Oh, you miserable cop! You didn't come to tell me this. You thought he might be here."

"I'm sure he isn't. This needn't be unpleasant."

"Why didn't you just ask me if he was here?"

"I figured you'd lie."

"No, you didn't. You were just embarrassed. When you knocked on the door you were praying I'd be dressed."

"I figure if Melvin came to you because he was in trouble, you'd protect him."

"You're saying I'd cheerfully become an accessory to murder."

239

"I don't think you'd necessarily be cheer-
ful."

"Chief, Melvin is a conniving son of a
bitch who always acts in his own best
interests. Committing a murder that will be
immediately tied to him in order to cover
up a murder that is only slightly tied to him
and most likely couldn't be proved is clearly
not in his best interests. Melvin is smart
enough to know that, and he wouldn't do
it."

"Is Melvin here?"

"No."

"You mind if I verify that?"

"I do. But I don't want to wait around
while you apply for a warrant. I'd like to get
on with my life. So feel free. If you could
try not to wake Jennifer up, I'd appreciate
it. She had a hot date last night and she's
tired."

"A date?"

"Some kid from class. Quite the lady's
man. Took her to McDonald's."

Aaron Grant wandered in in his pajamas.
"What's going on?"

"There's been another stabbing. Harper's
looking for Melvin."

"Here?"

"The chief doubts my virtue."

"Who's the victim?"

"Jason Tripp."

"The witness?"

"If you want to call him that. He wasn't a witness to the crime."

"The guy who saw Melvin put the knife in his car?"

"Melvin says he didn't."

"Well, it will be hard to prove now."

Harper came back.

"There's been another murder?" Aaron said.

"Yeah."

"A heads-up would have been nice."

"It's early."

"I bet Rick Reed got one."

"I have no control over what Dan Finley does."

"You're his boss."

"With regard to the job. I don't censor his speech."

"If Henry Firth wanted you to sit on something, you'd tell Dan to drop it fast enough. So who found it?"

"A clerk for Stop & Shop. Drove in for the early shift and there he was. Right behind the shopping carts."

"What time was that?"

"Five thirty."

"When you say early shift, you're not kidding around."

"Guy called us and set the wheels in motion. It's been a joyride ever since."

"Great," Cora said. "Now, if I'm not under arrest, I'd like to get dressed." She cocked her head at Aaron. "I make the chief uncomfortable in my nightgown."

CHAPTER 45

Becky wasn't happy to be called. "Yes?" she snarled. Cora figured she'd had a sleepless night.

"Wake up. There's been a murder."

"I know. I'm representing the defendant."

"Not that murder. There's been another."

"Who?"

Cora told her. Becky expressed her opinion in terms usually reserved for drill sergeants greeting the new recruits.

"I concur," Cora said. "Meet you at your office."

Cora finished dressing, hopped in the car, and drove downtown.

Becky was already there. "I can't get hold of my client."

"Join the club."

"Huh?"

"Chief Harper can't find him, either. I thought he was handing me a line. He thought I was handing him one. He came to my house looking for Melvin. I was less than pleased."

"I take it he wasn't there?"

"You want a fat lip?"

"What for?"

"Having to ask."

"I couched my question in the negative."

"Don't you know me better than that?"

"Figuring out your moods is never a sure thing."

"This is bad, Becky. The key witness against Melvin was killed last night, and he's disappeared."

"Did he sleep in his room?"

"I wouldn't know. Anyway, he's on the run, and it couldn't come at a worse time."

"So how are we going to find him?"

"I have no idea."

Melvin walked in the door. "Hi, kids. Wanna catch some breakfast?"

"Where the hell have you been?" Cora demanded.

"Don't get so huffy. You turned me down, remember?"

"You were with a girl?"

"You're not the only fish in the sea."

"Who was she?"

Melvin grinned. "That would be telling."

"No kidding. The police are going to be asking that question, and they're not going

244

to be too pleased with 'I'm too much of a gentleman to say.' If you don't say, Becky will be hard-pressed to save you, and she's damn good."

Melvin frowned. "What the hell's going on?"

"The key witness against you was killed last night," Becky said. "The police are looking for you. They're not very happy about it."

"What?"

Cora filled Melvin in on the details of the crime. It wasn't hard. There weren't many.

"This is not good," Melvin said.

"I think that's a brilliant assessment of the situation. Becky, would you concur?"

"You're going to have to give up the girl, Melvin."

Melvin made a face. "She's married."

"What a surprise," Cora said.

"Where was her husband at the time?"

"On a business trip."

"Well, that will help pin it down. Cora, you think you could find what residents are currently away on business?"

"Wouldn't it be better not to bring it up at all?" Melvin said.

"I'd hate to tell you your chances if you don't."

"Maybe I could come up with another alibi."

"I will not suborn perjury."

"I didn't say it wouldn't be true."

Becky took a breath. "All of that can wait. What can't wait is you have to go to the police right now. You're not on the run, you haven't taken flight, you're not avoiding anyone. The minute you heard, you went straight to the police."

"What do I tell them?"

"Nothing. I barge in and tell you not to talk. You find that frustrating. You didn't do anything, you're eager to talk, and your stodgy old lawyer won't let you."

"You're not that old."

Cora made a face. "Bad move, Melvin. Becky's been concerned about her age lately."

"I have not!" Becky snapped.

"See what I mean? I felt the same way when I turned forty."

"I am *not* forty."

"I didn't say you were. I said I felt that way then. See how sensitive she is?"

"I'm not sensitive. I want to get Melvin out of here before the cops swoop in and arrest him."

"You're sending me to the cops."

"Big difference who goes to whom."

"The old girl's right," Cora said. "Get out of here while the getting's good."

"If there's going to be a catfight, I'm not leaving."

"There's not going to be a catfight," Becky said.

"You say that now, but I know women."

"Get out of here."

"Come with me."

"No, you go alone. When you heard about this you didn't run to your lawyer, you went straight to the police."

"Won't that look stage-managed?"

"Sure, but they can't prove it."

"They'll ask me."

"Yes, but you won't tell them because it's been carefully stage-managed so your lawyer will show up."

"Works for me," Melvin said. He went out the door.

"How long you gonna give him?" Cora said.

"What do you think?"

Becky and Cora came down the stairs and reached the street just as Melvin was going up the steps to the police station.

"We should hurry," Cora said.

"You don't think Melvin can be discreet for thirty seconds?"

"He couldn't stay faithful to his wedding

vows for thirty seconds. The man has no self-control."

Becky picked up the pace. They walked into the police station just in time to hear Chief Harper say, "Where were you all night?"

"Why, Chief," Becky said. "Were you attempting to interrogate my client outside my presence? I didn't think you'd stoop to that."

"Your client has the right to remain silent. If he chooses not to exercise that right, he doesn't have to."

"Did he choose not to exercise that right?"

"He walked into the police station."

"I'm glad to hear you say so. I hope you'll remember that in case someone tries to claim he took to flight."

"I was just asking him where he was last night. I'm pleased to hear he wasn't on the lam."

"He wasn't."

"So where was he?"

"Nice try, Chief. When I saw Melvin go into the police station I knew he'd heard of the murder so I hurried to get here before he volunteered any information you aren't entitled to. It's lucky I got here in time."

"We make our own luck, don't we?" Chief Harper observed dryly.

"I don't know what you mean. Anyway, I can't let Melvin talk while he has a prosecution pending. If you'd care to dismiss the charge, it would be another matter."

"As if that might happen."

"That's what I thought. Sorry, Melvin. I know you'd like to cooperate, but I'm afraid I can't let you. So if you'd care to come along."

"That's not going to happen, either," Chief Harper said. "If Melvin's not going to cooperate, I have to hold him on suspicion of murder."

"He's on bail for that."

"Not for this one, he's not. You'll have to bail him out again. I've even heard tell of suspects on bail who commit a second crime who get that bail revoked."

"I'm glad my client hasn't done that. Of course, it's hard to commit a second crime if you haven't committed a first."

"I'm glad to see you're sharpening up your verbal skills," Chief Harper said. "It looks like you're going to need 'em. Meanwhile, Melvin's staying here."

CHAPTER 46

Becky stomped off to petition the judge for bail. Cora hung around to harangue Chief Harper. She paced the outer office impatiently while he locked Melvin up. Dan Finley was off chasing down clues, and there was no one to bother.

Finally, the chief came back out.

"Took you long enough," Cora grumbled. "Haven't you ever processed a prisoner before?"

"It's complicated with a serial killer. Much more paperwork. What'd you hang around for? Something you want to tell me?"

"I was going to ask you the same thing."

"The answer is no. I don't know any more than I did when I saw you at your house."

"I thought you might be able to concentrate better now that I'm dressed."

"You're not helping your cause."

"Wanna tell me what will?"

"A little frankness and honesty would be

refreshing."

"When have I not been frank and honest?"

"I tell you I'm looking for Melvin. Less than an hour later he walks into the police station."

"You're crabbing about that?"

"About your frankness and honesty claim. You told me you didn't know where he was."

"I didn't. I can't help it if you don't believe me, but it happens to be the truth."

"You didn't know where he was an hour ago, but you do now."

"So do you."

"What caused that change?"

"I have no idea."

"He just happened to turn up?"

"That's right."

"How'd that happen?"

"I don't know. I haven't had a chance to talk to him."

"Yeah, and you're not going to, either."

"That's not very nice. What did I do to deserve that?"

"I don't know, but I'm sure you did something. Can't you get that man out of your life? It's a disaster every time he turns up."

"I have no control over Melvin. Never did, never will."

"You were married to him."

"I rest my case."

"You must have some hold on him. He keeps showing up."

"I can't help it if I'm irresistible."

"Really, Cora, what's the deal?"

Cora glowered at him.

Chief Harper, suddenly embarrassed, fell all over himself. "I mean, that's not to say —"

Cora cut him off. "Let's talk about the crime."

"What about it?"

"The victim, for one thing."

"You know about him. He was the witness against Melvin."

"I was hoping we could discuss this in terms other than Melvin. I mean the victim himself. What's his deal?"

"He was one of the workers from the construction site. He was staying at the motel where —" Chief Harper caught himself just in time. "Where the other victim lived. He was at the same motel, he was on the same crew. Dan's questioning the construction crew now."

"So you don't know if the two were buddies? Hung out after work?"

"That's hard to establish when both parties are dead. You're talking thirdhand information well after the fact."

"Cry me a river. What about the time of death?"

"Barney's got the body now."

"He give you a preliminary?"

"He pronounced the guy dead."

"Come on, Chief, he's taken the temperature. What's the time frame?"

"Sorry. If Becky wants to be a hard-ass, I can be a hard-ass, too."

"This shouldn't be about horse trading."

"Yeah, but it always is. I don't think you're gonna change that."

"Good. You wanna talk about what you *can* talk about?"

"I can't even follow that."

"Sure you can. Aside from the things you feel richly inclined to be a hard-ass about, what can you tell me?"

"Nothing."

"You gonna be a hard-ass about everything?"

"No, I just don't have much. What I do's not for sale."

"Can I quote you on that, Chief? At the moment you're not able to sell any privileged information to the defense."

"You're not helping your cause."

"From what you say, that doesn't matter."

"That's right."

253

"Well, that's a conversation killer. You're not going to let me talk to Melvin?"

"In the lockup? Not a chance."

"I've done it before."

"Was that when you were cooperating with the police?"

"In what way am I not cooperating with the police?"

"You lied to me."

"Oh, come on. Just because you got it in your head I knew something and didn't tell you."

"Not just didn't tell me. You told me to my face you *didn't* know."

"And you decided I did, which settles the case. Luckily in a court of law these things aren't settled on a whim."

"We're not in a court of law. We're in my police station, where visiting prisoners in lockup is not a right but a privilege. You haven't earned that privilege. So you might as well run along."

"Yeah, I think I'll hang out until Becky gets back with the bail bond. Then we can talk to Melvin, and you can be the one who hasn't earned that privilege."

"I'm afraid Becky's not going to have much luck, either."

Cora frowned. "Why do you say that?"

"Judge Hobbs isn't going to sign off on

bail until the prosecutor weighs in."

"I'm sure he's on his way."

"He's in Cleveland."

"Cleveland?"

"Yeah. So even if he's on his way, it's going to be awhile before he gets here."

"What the hell is Ratface doing in Cleveland?"

"He's at a legal convention."

Cora felt like she'd been punched in the stomach.

CHAPTER 47

Becky walked into her office to find Cora sitting at her desk.

"We got trouble," Cora said.

"No kidding. I can't get Melvin out of jail."

Cora waved it away. "Small potatoes. He's better off *in* jail, where he can't get into trouble."

"What are you talking about?"

"I found the missing alibi witness."

"That's great!"

"No, it isn't."

"Why not?"

"It's Henry Firth's wife."

Becky sank down in the client chair. "Oh. My. God."

"That's right. Melvin has a death wish. He looks around for the most inappropriate woman possible, and he's gotta have her."

"How do you know?"

"I was married to him."

"How do you know it's Mrs. Firth?"

"You can't get him out of jail because the prosecutor isn't available. Ratface is at a convention in Cleveland. Melvin took advantage of the opportunity."

"Did you speak to him?"

"Chief Harper won't let me."

"You told him!"

"Don't be silly. He won't let me on general principles. He resents it when suspects out on bail kill again."

Becky sucked in her breath. "We're in trouble."

"I know. I didn't bury the lead. That's what I opened with."

"I gotta go see him."

"Why?"

"Find out what the hell he was thinking."

"Don't be stupid."

"What do you mean?"

"You know what he was thinking. Inasmuch as Melvin thinks about anything. The added kick of being the prosecutor's wife was just the icing on the cake."

"All right, I won't ask him."

"Can you do that?"

"What do you mean?"

"If you don't ask him who the woman is, he's going to smell a big, fat rat."

"A big, fat Ratface."

"I'm not sure he knows that nickname."
Becky shook her head and sighed heavily.
"This is terrible, Cora. This is the worst."
Cora nodded. "That's Melvin, all right."

CHAPTER 48

Sherry was at the computer when Cora got home.

"Hey, I got something," Sherry said.

"What?" Cora said grumpily.

"I know you're having a hard time. I was hoping I could come up with something for you."

"You want to lay it on me without the preamble."

"This isn't necessarily bad."

"You sound like my tax accountant."

"He saves us money."

"Yeah. He saves us twenty-five hundred and charges three grand. I fail to see the benefit."

"You don't understand finance."

"That's why. I don't care right now. I'm in a very bad mood."

"Because Melvin's in jail?"

"Don't be silly. I like him in jail."

"Right. You hate it when he's sleeping with

259

someone else. Is that it? Is he running around with a bimbo?"

"Not at the moment."

"Of course not. He's in jail. No wonder you don't mind."

"Melvin's on the hook for murder unless he can come up with an alibi witness for last night."

"And he doesn't have one?"

"No, he's got one. The woman he shacked up with."

"She won't testify?"

"We don't want her to."

"Why not?"

"It's Henry Firth's wife."

Sherry's mouth fell open. "Are you kidding me?"

"No. And I shouldn't even be telling you, because Melvin doesn't know we know."

"How do you know?"

"Melvin spent the night with a woman whose husband was away on business. Ratface was at a convention in Cleveland."

"That's all you've got to go on?"

"It's Melvin. Can you think of anything that would please him more?"

"Getting back together with you."

"I'm not talking fantasy here. This is real life. So, what have you got?"

"I know this couldn't interest you less, I

was working on the crossword puzzle and I came up with something."

"You're right, this couldn't interest me less."

"You want to hear this or not?"

"Okay. Go on."

"I found the word CENTER clued as 'midpoint,' and FIVE clued as 'prime number.' "

"So?"

"Prime number is a gimme. The answer has four letters. There's only one prime number that's four letters long: 'five.' "

"Couldn't the answer be something else?"

"What do you mean?"

"I don't know, because I can't do crosswords. But a person who *can*, like you, could say, a prime number could also be a clue for, and come up with some mathematical term that means the same thing as a prime number."

"There's no such thing."

"As a prime number? Then what are we talking about?"

"Are you *trying* to be a pain in the ass?"

"I don't know. Maybe. So you figure this is the connection Peggy wanted us to find?"

"No, I don't."

"Why not?"

"Because the clues aren't in the puzzle

Peggy gave us."

"What the hell are you talking about?"

"The clues are in the puzzle you found in her truck."

"Whoops."

"Yeah. The clues are in the wrong puzzle."

"How could it be the wrong puzzle? You solved it. Harvey Beerbaum solved it. I taunted Chief Harper with it: 'you say yes, some say no.' "

"Yeah, but it's not the puzzle that refers to the Sudoku. If it does, and this is not just a monumental coincidence, somehow or other someone got the puzzles mixed up and you wound up with the wrong one."

"Sherry, you're making this up. Yes, you have the word 'five.' And, yes, you have the word 'center.' There's no reason to assume they refer to a Sudoku at all."

"That's what *I* thought. So I did some checking. I'm assuming — and don't remind me what assuming makes of you and me — I'm taking as a hypothesis 'center' would refer to the center row going across, and 'five' would refer to the five numbers in the middle of that row. The five numbers in this puzzle are six, four, three, nine, two."

"Fascinating."

"Hey, don't shoot the messenger. So I started looking around for what that number might be. Too short to be a phone number or Social Security number. Unlikely to be a combination lock number."

"Well, that's obvious. You mind telling me what it *is* likely to be?"

"A license plate number. Unfortunately, I'm not set up to trace license plate numbers. Fortunately, I know an investigative reporter."

"Rick Reed?"

"Aaron, you putz. You did that deliberately. Anyway, hubby came through with a name."

"What name?"

"Johnny Dawson."

CHAPTER 49

Cora sat staring back and forth from the puzzle to the Sudoku. "I see it, but I don't believe it."

"I figured it out, but I don't believe it."

"How could this have happened?"

"That's your department. I just do the puzzles."

"Damn it, Sherry, help me out. My head is coming off here. It's like A follows B, but it doesn't, it actually follows C. And C is ahead of A, because someone accidentally switched the labels."

"Labels?"

"Go with it, I'm improvising."

"Is that the same as freaking out?"

"In this case, yes. If the Sudoku goes with the second puzzle, and the second puzzle should be the first puzzle, then there's no reason to believe either puzzle has anything to do with Melvin at all. Johnny Dawson could just as well be the guy about whom they're asking, *Did he do it?*"

"Anybody could."

"Exactly. It's generic. It's only when you throw in this fantastic license plate theory of yours."

"You're the math whiz. What's the probability of a five-digit number matching Johnny's license plate?"

"Ask the guys who play the lottery. It's a hundred thousand to one. Not the type of odds you'd like to base a defense strategy on."

"This is good news, Cora. If I'm right, the puzzles have nothing to do with Melvin at all."

A car rolled up the driveway. Cora and Sherry went to the window. It was actually a truck. Peggy Dawson jumped out and ran up the driveway, waving a paper.

"Well, this should be interesting," Sherry said.

"Not the word I would have used."

"Want me to solve the puzzle or tell her where to stick it?"

"You know my choice."

"I wonder if it's a crossword or a Sudoku. If it's a Sudoku, I wonder if it has *Melvin's* license number."

"He's in a rental car."

"So? It's not like this was planned in

advance. The guy barely hit town when it all went to hell."

"Yeah. That's Melvin's MO," Cora said. As Peggy got closer, she added, "It's a crossword."

"Try to keep the delight out of your voice."

"It's another crossword," Peggy said. "I knew there would be."

"Why?"

"To go with the Sudoku."

"You thought it went with the other puzzle."

"Here." Peggy thrust the puzzle at Cora.

"Why aren't you bringing this to Harvey Beerbaum?"

"You solved the Sudoku."

"And that's why I didn't want to. You solve one puzzle, and you're fair game. Where'd you get this one?"

"It was outside my door."

"Someone snuck up to your room and left a crossword puzzle in the hall?"

"What's wrong with that?"

"It's unusual behavior."

"We've had two murders. What's *not* unusual?"

"She's got you there," Sherry said.

Cora glowered at her.

"I'm afraid you're going to have to take

this to Harvey Beerbaum," Sherry said. "I'll scan a copy in case it comes to anything."

Peggy reluctantly gave up the puzzle. She wasn't happy to have it in anyone's hands but Cora's.

Sherry was back in minutes. "Here you go. Run along to Harvey's. If he comes up with anything, you can call us from there, you don't have to come back."

"That's so silly. Couldn't you just do it now?"

"No, I can't," Cora said. "Come on, kid. How'd you feel if your boyfriend was the one in jail?"

"That would be awful."

"Yeah. So unless you have an unhealthy May-December relationship with the suspect, you got nothing to worry about."

"I keep getting puzzles."

"There's no proof the puzzles have anything to do with the murders."

Peggy stomped her foot and flounced down the walk.

"Did you solve the puzzle?" Cora said as Peggy drove off.

"I was only gone a minute."

"So solve it now."

"I don't have to."

"Why not?"

"It's the same one."

"What?"

"It's the same as the one we have."

"She gave me a copy of the same puzzle and didn't even notice?"

"Not that puzzle. She gave you a copy of the one you found in her truck."

"That makes no sense at all."

"What else is new?"

"Someone left a crossword in her truck. When she didn't find it, because I stole it, they left a copy in front of her door."

"Apparently so."

"Well, I don't buy it."

"Why not?"

"The puzzle in her truck was folded up and slid down the side pocket in the door. Where no one would expect her to find it. And the other one is left in plain sight."

"It wouldn't be the first time someone needed a hint."

"Hold on a minute."

"What?"

"This is the one with the five and the center?"

"Right."

"The one that points to her brother?"

"If you believe the license plate clue."

"I didn't before, but I do now. This is getting freaky."

"Gonna tell Chief Harper?"

"Let's let Harvey Beerbaum."

"What if he doesn't figure it out?"

"I might have to help him. That's what Chief Harper will expect me to do. Step in and make sense of everything."

"Failing that, you can give him the license plate number."

"Thanks a bunch. Yes, I can give him the license plate number, but there's no hurry about it."

"You think that's going to satisfy Peggy?"

"Who knows what satisfies Peggy? She doesn't seem too upset her boyfriend got killed. Not to mention her source of crack."

"That's right. She didn't seem concerned about anything but the stupid puzzle."

Cora spread her arms to the heavens. "Thank you, gods. I shall long remember this day. My niece, the super puzzle nerd, has just referred to a puzzle as stupid."

CHAPTER 50

"If I tell you something, you promise not to use it?"

Becky looked at Cora suspiciously. "Why?"

"You have a client. You're bound to act in his best interests."

"Yes, I am."

"It's early in the case yet. It's hard to know what your client's best interests are."

"How bad is this?"

"It's not bad. It's good. I think it will eventually help you. Just not now."

"I'm intrigued. And why would it be in my client's best interests to betray my client?"

"Who said anything about betraying? I'm talking about *preserving* your client's best interests. By giving him the optimal chance to take advantage of the evidence as it presents itself."

"What is it?"

"You recall that crossword puzzle I found in Peggy Dawson's truck?"

"I recall *all* your illegal searches and seizures."

"Technically, isn't it the police who do that? I'm a private citizen."

"The more you stall, the worse this sounds. What about the puzzle?"

"Peggy Dawson gave me another one."

"We have *three* puzzles?"

"Only if we wanna count the Sudoku. Which it turns out we do."

"We don't have three crosswords?"

"No."

"What's wrong with my math?"

"Peggy has happily presented me with a copy of the one I found in her truck."

"Run that by me again."

"She clearly didn't know I had it. She gave me another. She claimed it was left outside the door."

"Of her truck?"

"Of her room."

"I fail to see how this helps my client."

"It doesn't. Forget I said anything."

"Cora."

"Peggy Dawson had a theory that the crossword relates to the Sudoku. The first one doesn't. The one she just gave me does."

"In what way does it relate to the Su-

271

doku?" Becky said, clearly holding herself back with effort.

"This is where we need to be careful."

"If you don't tell me how it does, there's going to be another homicide. I'm sure it will be justifiable."

"Sherry noticed that two of the answers in the puzzle, taken together, could be construed to mean the five numbers in the center of the Sudoku."

"And how does this help my client?"

"That depends on who your client is."

"Cora."

"You've already had two clients in this case. The evidence against Melvin isn't strong. The worst thing the prosecutor has on him is going to bed with his wife. Take that away and the case is a breeze."

"The knife in his car notwithstanding."

"The knife was planted. You know it, I know it, I'm sure the police know it."

"You base your opinion on the fact they arrested Melvin?"

"They also arrested Johnny Dawson. They're not particular. They'll take anyone they think they can prosecute."

"What did Sherry find?"

"You promise you won't do anything for five minutes?"

"Why five minutes?"

"I'm trying to save you from a knee-jerk reaction."

"And why do I need saving?"

"You want this information or not?"

"Five minutes. Go."

"The five numbers in the center of the Sudoku are Johnny Dawson's license plate." Becky looked at her watch.

"That's the wrong way to take it."

"What's the right way? You just negotiated five extra minutes of incarceration for your ex-husband. But that's all you got."

"No, it's not. Because you're not so stupid as to throw away a perfectly good defense strategy just for the sake of getting your client out of jail."

"Isn't that the point?"

"The point is to prevent him from getting a jail sentence, not postpone it. Anyway, it's not going to work. Even if Chief Harper believes you, and that's a big if, Henry Firth won't. Even if he were here, which he's not. And he's not going to sanction letting Melvin out, even if he doesn't know he's been boffing his wife."

"You have any other words of encouragement?"

"The best this does is give you reasonable doubt. You don't want reasonable doubt now. If you ever go to trial, that's when

273

you'll need it."

"Who knows about this?"

"Just us and Sherry. Oh, and Aaron."

"Aaron?"

"He's not going to write it."

"How do you know?"

"Because he's happily married. And that would end it. So he's sitting on it. Though he is a bit frustrated."

"I thought frustrated married men were your specialty."

"Not my niece's. Come on, Becky. Think this through."

"Peggy brought you this?"

"Yes."

"But you didn't tell her what Sherry found?"

"Hell, no. I didn't even let on I knew what the puzzle says."

"Harvey may figure it out."

"Harvey's a stodgy twit. Seeing connections between word and number puzzles is hardly his forte."

Becky frowned.

"Ah," Cora said. "Logic has begun to set in."

"If Harvey figures it out and goes to the police, there's nothing we can do."

"Granted. But unlikely."

"You say Peggy's pushing the theory?"

"Yes."

"Then she'll push it with Harvey."

"So?"

"She could prod him into action."

"I wish you hadn't said that. The image will be forever seared in my memory."

"Seriously, Cora, I don't trust that girl."

"You don't trust a teenage crack addict? I can't see why not."

"She's got an agenda. And she'll keep on pushing until she gets it."

"What's her agenda?"

"To keep her brother out and keep Melvin in."

"In that case she's not going to like what she finds."

"Or what she makes Harvey Beerbaum find. And I can't see him tracing license plate numbers."

"He wouldn't."

"Right. So she'll push him to give the number to Chief Harper. Who'll have no trouble whatsoever tracing it as a license plate and coming up with Johnny Dawson."

"Right, and since Peggy won't know that when she prods Harvey to go to the police, she'll have no braking system keeping her from doing it until it turns out to be Johnny's plate. The beauty of this is it won't be the defense bringing it to the police, it will be the police bringing it to us."

"If they choose to do so."

"And if they don't choose to do so?"

"Then Peggy will bring it to us."

"Why would they tell her?"

"They wouldn't. Then she'll be demanding to know. And demanding we find out. And demanding Harvey Beerbaum finds out. Hell, she might even get her brother to demand she finds out. Wouldn't that be ironic?"

Becky frowned. "This doesn't help us at all."

"That's what I've been trying to tell you."

CHAPTER 51

Aaron wasn't happy. "You know, it's no fun always being a nice guy."

"You can't help it, Aaron," Cora said. "That's who you are."

"That's who I'm constantly forced to be. Generally I'm caught between you and Sherry and the *Bakerhaven Gazette*. You know what place the *Gazette* comes in?"

"It's a nonstory, Aaron. It doesn't mean what you think it does."

"I don't know what it means. I just know I have it and I can't write it. And it must mean something, or I *would* be able to write it."

"There's reverse logic, if I ever heard it."

"What's so important about Johnny Dawson? I thought the police cleared him of the crime."

"They didn't clear him of the crime. They just got someone better."

"Melvin's better?"

"Much. He's an outsider with ties to me. He had a motive and the murder weapon. In the other case, he had an even stronger motive. Johnny Dawson began to look like a bad bet."

"But he isn't?"

"You need more facts for the story you can't write?"

"From what you tell me, it's a big story."

"It's a big story that you don't want to write. What's your angle? The Bakerhaven police are prosecuting the wrong man because it will be a flashier case? That's not going to make you very popular. And on what evidence do you base this wild claim? The knife Johnny turned in with the blood on it that didn't match the victim's? Or the fact you're married to my niece and Melvin is my ex-husband?"

Aaron frowned. "Sherry wouldn't tell me where the license plate number came from. I assume that's a big clue in itself."

"The license number came from a crossword. Not to mention a Sudoku."

"A Sudoku?"

"I told you not to mention that."

"Where did the puzzles come from?"

"I know where the police are going to say they came from."

"Where?"

"Me. I made 'em up to help Melvin."

"Because they don't realize you *couldn't* make 'em up, and helping Melvin has never been a high priority."

"Right. Though framing him for murder never occurred to me before."

"Do the police know about the puzzle?"

"Absolutely. Harvey Beerbaum's solving it now. If they come up with Johnny Dawson, they're not going to be pleased."

"If they come up with Johnny Dawson, I can write the story."

"Anything you learn from independent sources is fair game. We can't have Rick Reed spouting off about it and you pretending it doesn't exist. If you come out first it not only looks bad, it automatically reveals your sources."

"So I can't have an exclusive but you'll graciously allow me to print what you're giving everybody else."

Cora smiled and shrugged. "Couldn't have said it better."

CHAPTER 52

Cora drove by the real estate office. Johnny Dawson's car was parked out front. She pulled off to the side of the road and settled down to wait.

She was in luck. Johnny was out ten minutes later, looking like someone killed his cat. He hopped in his car, drove straight to the police station, and stormed in.

Cora was right on his heels. She wouldn't have missed this for the world.

Johnny strode up to Dan Finley and stuck an accusing finger in his face. "You're questioning my sister!"

The young officer looked up from his desk. "Not at the moment, I'm not."

Cora stifled a laugh.

Johnny's face got red. "You think it's funny, picking on a teenage girl?"

"No one's picking on her."

"You pulled her truck over and questioned her. Talk about intimidation. Turned on your flashing lights and pulled her right off the road."

"This is a murder investigation, as you well know."

"What's that supposed to mean? If it means you were stupid enough to arrest me on a whim, I quite agree. My lawyer's thinking of filing suit for false arrest."

Becky was thinking no such thing. Cora wasn't even sure she was Johnny's lawyer anymore.

"Why did you pull my sister off the road? Flashing your lights like she'd done something wrong. You know how scary that is for a teenage girl?"

Cora couldn't imagine Peggy was very scared. Of course she might have been high on drugs, and the sight of a police car freaked her out.

Dan Finley wasn't taking any guff from Johnny Dawson. He got up and came around his desk. "I'm sorry you're upset. Yes, I questioned your sister. I questioned *lots* of people. Someone at the construction site mentioned the victim being picked up by a girl in a truck. That sounded like Peggy. So I tracked her down and questioned her. She finally admitted it was."

"Finally admitted?"

"After she realized I knew it was her

anyway. Look, Mr. Dawson, I'm sure there was nothing untoward about the relationship. They'd never been out on a date, never been to his motel. She claims they just liked to hang out. Just between you and me, I think she was doing a little detective work. It shook her up when you got arrested. Even now that you're off the hook she wants to know. I think she's just making sure."

"That's what you got from pulling her off the road?"

"That's right."

"Was it worth it?"

"What?"

"Scaring a teenage girl to death for that information. Was it worth it? Did it speed your investigation along?"

"Ninety percent of police work is ruling things out."

"And the other ten percent is arresting the wrong people."

Dan let Johnny have the last word. He turned and went back to his desk.

Johnny glared at him for emphasis, then stomped out the door.

CHAPTER 53

Cora was stuck. If she didn't leave, she'd lose him. If she did leave, Dan Finley would know she was following him. That might result in questions she wasn't prepared to answer.

She smiled, sauntered over to Dan's desk. "Hey, Dan, how's it going?"

"You heard that?"

"Hard to miss. You picking on young girls now?"

Dan grimaced. "When I started this job, they didn't seem that young. Now it's like I'm a big, bad cop."

"Yeah, tough as nails," Cora said. "You really question his sister?"

"Link to the decedent. Not a big link, but there aren't many. Guy's from the City. Most of the crew are. Brought in for the job, don't know anybody."

"The foreman couldn't hire local talent?"

"Not with any experience. High school

kids looking for something to put on a college résumé, college kids looking for something in their field, graduates looking to leave town. Not many looking to make the construction crew. Or to make cop, for that matter."

"You sound bitter, Dan. You're too young to be bitter."

"I'm glad I'm too young for something. So whaddya want? If it's to see Melvin, I have strict instructions to the contrary."

"I want a lead, Dan. I want some sort of a lead. I got a case that doesn't make any sense with Melvin in the middle. That's my least favorite kind."

"The chief still thinks you were hiding Melvin at your house."

Cora sighed. "I wasn't hiding Melvin at my house. I happen to know Melvin didn't do it. But as long as the cops think so, we have a huge disconnect. I'd like to find something to change their minds."

"Hey, I'm a cop."

"Then help me change your mind. You're not so jaded as to not care about convicting an innocent man."

"Melvin's innocent?"

Cora waggled her hand. "Bad choice of words. Let's just say he didn't do it, and leave it at that."

"I don't think that's where we're apt to leave it."

"Yeah. So what you told Johnny Dawson about his sister."

"What about it?"

"Was it true?"

"Absolutely."

"You leave anything out?"

"Not really."

"What do you mean, not really?"

"One of the guys on the crew thought the guy might be sweet on her."

"Sweet on her? How quaint."

"Yeah. Everyone else pooh-poohed it, and the guy wasn't sure. Of course they might have just pooh-poohed it because she was underage."

"Worried about getting the dead guy in trouble? You got anything else?"

Dan hesitated. "If I say yes, you'll want to know what it is. If I say no, you'll tell Becky the police have nothing, and she'll start taunting us in the press."

"Well, let's put it this way. Is any part of the monumental volume of information the police have gathered on the crime something you feel that you can share?"

"Nicely framed."

"Nicely enough to be worthy of an answer?"

285

"Well, for one thing, we've had complaints about drugs connected to people on the crew."

"What kind of drugs?"

"No one knew. It was very nonspecific. Just the kind of complaint we get when people come in from the City."

"My native land. I'm very proud."

"And Sam Brogan searched Peggy's truck for traces of blood. He didn't find any."

"Did she put up a squawk about that?"

"She didn't know. He did it when I had her in for questioning."

"I thought you questioned her by the side of the road."

"I pulled her over to say we needed to talk. I didn't make her sit in the police car. I let her drive back to the station."

"Always the gentleman."

"Yeah."

"Was she grateful?"

"Not so you'd notice."

"Teenagers don't trust the police."

"At what age do they grow out of it?"

"That's unkind, Dan. I always trusted you. Even when you were arresting me, I could always count on you to be fair."

"I can feel the gut punch coming. What are you leading up to, Cora?"

"Absolutely nothing." Cora took a breath.

"So. You're not allowed to let me talk to Melvin."

"I knew this was coming."

"So you're prepared."

"I'm prepared to say no."

"This doesn't have to get nasty."

"Nothing nasty about it. I'm being perfectly pleasant."

"I'm sure you'll get a gold star."

Cora left the police station and looked up and down Main Street, just in case Johnny Dawson had stopped to get coffee and a muffin on his way out of town, but it was no use.

Johnny Dawson was gone.

CHAPTER 54

Cora poked her head in the door of Becky's office. "Good news, bad news."

"What's the bad news?"

"I lost Johnny Dawson."

"And the good news?"

"Dan Finley doesn't know I was following him."

"Is there a connection?"

"That's right."

"Now that I'm emotionally prepared, lay it on me."

"Johnny went to the police station. I followed him in to see what he was doing there. I couldn't follow him out, or Dan Finley would have known I was following him. So I hung around, convinced him I was trying to get in to see Melvin."

"Did you get in?"

"No. That's what made it convincing."

"I don't know if it was worth losing Johnny."

"It is if you don't want it to be a parade. If the cops figure out we're tailing Johnny, *they'll* start tailing Johnny. You won't be able to turn around without bumping into a tail."

"Why did Johnny go to the police station?"

"Lodge a complaint about the cops hassling his sister. Cops found out she was a friend of the decedent. Dan Finley pulled her over to ask her about it."

"Pulled her over?"

"Said the lawyer, practically drooling at the prospect of litigation."

"How bad *was* the roadside stop?"

"He stopped her for no apparent reason. He turned on the flashing lights."

"What's Johnny planning to do about it?"

"Stamp his foot real hard and say it isn't fair."

Becky nodded. "That's usually effective. It's a wonder the girl has time to run around with crossword puzzles."

"Not to mention crack pipes. The cops heard rumors about drugs among the work crew."

"What are they doing about it?"

"Keeping their kids away, I guess. They're not investigating it."

"They're not investigating it?"

"They got a murder to deal with. Two, at

last count."

"How they coming with that?"

"They think they solved it."

"Come on. It practically screams frame-up."

"Why is that?"

"It's Melvin. Everything about him is phony. An arrest for murder seems out of his league."

"Hey. Hey. The guy hit on you a few times. There's no reason to beat him up."

"And of course you defend him."

"What's that supposed to mean?"

"This is why battered wives can't leave their husbands."

"I am not a battered wife. Melvin isn't a wife beater, either. Sherry's first husband was. I know the difference."

There was a knock on the door and Aaron Grant came in. "Hi, guys. Wanna know where Johnny Dawson is?"

CHAPTER 55

Aaron sat down and casually crossed his legs. He seemed to enjoy the fact Becky and Cora were staring at him.

"What the hell?" Cora said.

"Johnny Dawson. I figured you'd be looking for him long about now. Wanna let me in on the discussion, or are you still excluding the pesky reporter?"

"Start talking or I'll break your head," Cora said.

"Who could resist such a charming invitation? Okay, I followed him since early this morning. I saw you pick him up at the real estate office. That must have been a token appearance, because he wasn't there long. I saw you follow him into the police station. I saw him come out alone. I figured you were trapped because you wouldn't want the police to know you were tailing him."

Cora's mouth was open. "I never saw you."

"Well, that's the thing about clandestine surveillance."

"Oh, listen to the big-time investigative reporter showing off in front of the hot young lawyer."

Aaron flushed. "That's not what I was doing."

"Hey, get over it," Becky said. "Tell us what you got."

"Johnny went out to the construction site. Had a talk with the crew. He wasn't happy."

"What did he say?"

"I couldn't get close enough to hear. Not without flashing my press pass and announcing my presence. But I was able to get the gist."

"Which was?"

"The guys should lay off his sister, she's underage."

"That couldn't have been very popular."

"It wasn't. I could see the crew closing ranks."

"But there was no physical confrontation?"

"No. But it had to shake them up. Particularly if they were involved with his sister."

Aaron cocked his head and smiled. "So. Do I have to sit on *this* story?"

"Where's Johnny now?" Cora said. "You just let him get away?"

"He's showing a house. I don't want to see a house. If you're interested, it's out on Sunset. I figure he's through doing anything interesting and has returned to actual work. The police station and the construction site seem to have been his only targets. Unless you got something else I should be looking into, I'm done."

"We don't," Becky said. "Cora's just cranky because she didn't spot you."

"I'm not cranky," Cora said irritably. "But I'd like to get something done."

"Like what?"

"Well, how about drugs on the crew? There's a criminal activity the police are ignoring."

"You're telling me to write about it. How would I presume to know?"

"You're an investigative reporter. You protect your sources."

"*I'm* my source."

"Then I think you'd want to do a good job."

"It's a tough story."

"Why?"

"Well, it's either connected to the murder, or it isn't."

"I would say that's a safe bet."

"No, I'm serious. What's my angle?"

"Oh, for goodness' sakes, do I have to

write your story for you? Drugs are connected to the crew, and both murdered men were on it."

"He's just goading you, Cora. You think Aaron doesn't know how to write a story?"

Aaron's eyes were twinkling. "It's hardly fair. I'd never get away with it if she weren't distracted by Melvin."

Before Cora could explode, Dan Finley pushed his way through the door. He didn't look happy.

"Cora Felton. I have a warrant for your arrest."

CHAPTER 56

Becky at tempted to act as Cora's attorney, but Cora was having none of it. The concept of the right to remain silent was somehow lost on her. Cora had opinions to express, whether or not they might be used in evidence against her, and she wasn't about to miss a chance to express those sentiments over something as silly as going to jail.

"What is she charged with?" Becky said, when she was able to get a word in edgewise.

"Fabricating evidence, obstructing justice, interfering with a police investigation, and conspiring to conceal a crime," Chief Harper said.

Dan Finley had marched Cora into the police station, despite Rick Reed trying to block their way with a camera. It was a small miracle Dan had managed to elude him. It had been one hell of a photo op.

"Chicken feed," Becky said. "If you're not going to charge her with murder, I don't know why we're talking. Most of my clients are A-list offenders."

"It isn't funny, Becky," Chief Harper said. "This time Cora's gone too far."

"She hasn't gone anywhere. She was sitting in my office minding her own business when Dan came and got her."

"He didn't do that on a whim. I have reason and allegation to believe she planted evidence in this case."

"Why would she do that?"

"In order to get her ex-husband out of jail by framing someone else for the crime."

"Have you met my ex-husband?" Cora said sarcastically.

"There's no love lost between them, believe me," Becky said. "Cora's more likely to *frame* her ex-husband for the crime."

"That's for show, Becky. You know they like each other."

"Hey. I'm sitting right here," Cora said.

Chief Harper wasn't amused. "The evidence is pretty conclusive, Becky. Peggy Dawson brought in a crossword puzzle."

"That's hardly my fault, Chief," Cora said. "I told her to give it to Harvey Beerbaum."

"She also brought in a Sudoku."

"I don't care if she brought in a copy of *Crime and Punishment*," Becky said. "It has

296

nothing to do with my client."

"Harvey solved the puzzle and the Sudoku."

"Could you expect less?"

"He also had a theory about what they meant."

"I'd be surprised if he didn't," Cora said. "How does it relate to me?"

"Have you solved the puzzle?"

"I can honestly say that I haven't."

"For your information, the theme entry is an enigmatic rhyme that appears meaningless. But Harvey also found entries in the puzzle that could relate to a Sudoku."

Cora looked up. "Harvey did? I'm shocked."

"According to Harvey, the puzzle pointed to five numbers in the Sudoku. We examined those numbers for significance. They turned out to be Johnny Dawson's license plate number."

"And this is somehow *my* fault? I assure you, Chief, I didn't write the puzzles, I didn't solve the puzzles, I have no *idea* who came up with those puzzles, but it certainly wasn't me."

"You didn't plant them in Peggy Dawson's truck?"

"What?"

"It's been charged that you planted this

297

evidence in Peggy Dawson's truck in order to implicate her brother and get your ex-husband off the hook."

Becky inserted herself between Cora and Chief Harper.

"Charged by whom?"

"County Prosecutor Henry Firth. He's particularly displeased. He's charged Cora with all the counts I just read."

Cora put up her hand. "This is all a misunderstanding, Chief."

Becky cut her off. "Yes, it is. And one that we will straighten out without petty wrangling. I will talk this over with my client, you will talk this over with the prosecutor, a meeting of minds will be reached, and we will be able to point out the error of your ways. I can only say if this is the extent of your evidence, your allegation was premature, to say the least."

"But it's not," Chief Harper said. "You see, there's a witness."

"To what?"

"A witness who saw Cora putting the puzzles in the truck."

Becky laughed and shook her head. "This is just absurd. You also have a witness who saw Melvin putting the murder weapon in his rental car. As well as witnesses who saw Melvin having two separate altercations with one of the murdered men. Who are those witnesses? Men from the same construction crew the victims worked on. Anytime they get in trouble they get together, and, poof, a new witness shows up. I assume you have someone from the construction crew who saw Cora searching Peggy's truck."

"I wish it were that simple," Chief Harper said.

"Why isn't it?"

"The witness isn't someone from the construction crew."

"Well, who is it?"

"Judy Douglas Knauer."

CHAPTER 57

"That scheming bitch!" Cora said.

"Easy. Take it easy."

"Melvin worked his wiles on her, and she's out to discredit me."

"That makes no sense."

"It makes perfect sense. Weren't you ever in love? We've got to get you dating. You can't be a stuffy lawyer all the time. You may make big bucks, but what's the point?"

"I *don't* make big bucks."

"Then what's the point?"

"Cora, you protest a bit too much. You're also running off at the mouth, so I can't get a word in edgewise."

They were in the interrogation room. Becky had managed to muscle Cora in before she blabbed much in front of Chief Harper. It hadn't been easy. A betrayal by a close friend, a bridge partner, no less, was more offensive to Cora than the actual arrest, and she had a lot to say. Preventing her from saying it was becoming a full-time job.

"Wouldn't you like to know the details?" Becky said.

"Details? There's no details. Judy says I planted the puzzle. I didn't plant the puzzle. End of story. Who you gonna believe, your client or some conniving real estate broker?"

"I thought Judy was your friend."

"You really have to start dating. You're starting to sound like a Barbie doll."

"Cora, snap out of it. You may find it hard to believe, but the whole world is not hung up on Melvin. Assume you don't know Judy, Judy doesn't know you, this is just a random stranger making that statement. If she has no agenda, how could she make that mistake?"

"That doesn't prove she's got an agenda?"

Becky shook her head. "It's a wonder you ever solve anything."

"How can I solve anything if I'm in jail?"

"The other night, when you dropped me off in town, you were gung-ho to hide the receipt for the knife in Peggy Dawson's truck."

"And you told me not to, so I didn't."

"Because you defer to me in all matters and follow my instructions to the letter."

"Because I realized it was a bad idea. Not

301

to mention the fact you'd know I'd done it."

"Before you got all virtuous, how close did you come to hiding it?"

"I was never close to hiding it. It was a stupid idea and I never entertained it."

"Now I know you're lying."

"You're a lawyer. You're supposed to believe your clients."

"Only if I'm stupid. Clients lie. That's why they're clients."

"Since when was I a client? I thought I was your investigator."

"You're the one who called yourself a client. If you can't come up with a better explanation, I can't get you out of jail."

"Can you recommend a lawyer who could?"

"Houdini might have a chance."

"Did he pass the bar?"

"Seriously. Do you have an explanation that will satisfy the chief?"

"I can't come up with one that will satisfy Henry Firth, and that's what we're talking about here. Chief Harper says Ratface isn't happy. Do you suppose he found out about his wife?"

"Shh! Don't even think that."

"Oh, that's your advice? Hide my head in the sand and hope they haven't come up with all the damning evidence?"

"That's not evidence. It's prejudicial material."

"Prejudicial enough to make Henry Firth recuse himself?"

"Only if I bring it up and prove it. Can you imagine that hearing?"

"So what's your plan?"

Becky got up. "I'll see what I can do."

"What about *me*?" Cora cried in exasperation.

Becky smiled. "Why don't you hang out here?"

CHAPTER 58

Melvin smiled. "I knew you'd find a way."

"What are you talking about?"

"To get to see me. When I heard they weren't letting you in, I said to myself, that won't last long. Just couldn't stay away, could you?"

"I didn't get arrested just to see you."

"Why not? It's mild compared to some other things you've done."

"I don't even *want* to see you."

"Well, that's not true, is it? How could you be denied access if you weren't trying to get in?"

"I may have asked to talk to you. It wasn't the end of the world when I found out I couldn't."

"You wanted to talk to me. How sweet."

"I'm working for your attorney, trying to figure out how you got arrested for a crime you didn't commit."

"You think I'm innocent. What loyalty."

"Oh, bite me. The general consensus is you haven't got the balls to do it."

"You'd like me to kill someone to prove my manhood?" Melvin grinned. "You know, when Dan marched you in here, I thought you'd arranged for a conjugal visit."

"Now you're just being pathetic."

"Try desperate. You know how long I've been in here?"

"It just seems long, Melvin, because you can't wait to get out. Wait'll you're convicted and awaiting execution. The days will just fly by."

"I'm glad to hear it," Melvin said. "What is it you're accused of doing?"

"Planting evidence to get you out."

"That is so nice of you."

"I didn't do it, you idiot."

"It's all right. I don't think the cells are wired."

"I'm not saying I didn't do it because I think the cells are wired, I'm saying I didn't do it because I didn't do it."

Melvin nodded approvingly. "Excellent. Did Becky tell you to say that?"

"I don't know why I bother to talk to you."

"What evidence did you plant?"

"I didn't plant any evidence."

"Sorry. What evidence do they *think* you planted?"

"A crossword puzzle and a Sudoku."

"That *sounds* like you."

"I swear I'm going to rip your face off."

"And what did this crossword puzzle say?"

"According to Harvey Beerbaum, it gave a strong hint the police should be looking at Johnny Dawson."

"Harvey Beerbaum said that? Boy, the heavyweights are lining up on my side." Melvin put up his hand. "That's not to imply that you're a heavyweight."

"It couldn't matter less, Melvin. No one's buying it. Everyone thinks I did it. When in point of fact I'd rather *frame* you for a crime than trump up an alibi to get you off."

"An alternate killer isn't really an alibi, now, is it? More like a reasonable hypothesis other than guilt, or however that swimsuit model of a lawyer would put it. So how did the puzzle point to Johnny Dawson?"

"I thought you might to like to know. Unless you're just trying to make me *think* you want to know to cover up the fact you *already* know because you constructed the damn thing yourself."

"Perish the thought," Melvin said. "We can't *all* be good at constructing crosswords, now, can we?"

Cora felt a chill. There it was. The implicit threat. If she didn't cooperate, he'd spill the beans. Just the sort of thing he'd say when he already intended to spill the beans and her cooperation had nothing to do with it.

"The puzzle was a nonsense poem about something being a bother. Rather appropriate, don't you think? If anything ever was a bother, you are. And getting arrested is certainly a bother. And that damn Dawson girl is the biggest bother of them all. I swear, she's been at me like a gnat, ever since she gave me the first crossword. I swat her away, and she comes right back."

"You want me to take care of her for you?"

"Aside from the fact you're in jail and can't do anything, were you offering to seduce a sixteen-year-old girl or have her whacked?"

"Which would you prefer?"

"It doesn't matter. I wouldn't count on going anywhere soon."

"Why do you say that?"

"Your choice of sleeping companion. I found your alibi witness, Melvin, and it isn't pretty. Not the woman herself, I suppose she's fine, but her husband leaves a lot to be desired, particularly when one's up for murder. I wouldn't expect to be catching a break anytime soon."

"Oops," Melvin said.

"Yeah. Oops. Did you do that accidentally,

or for an added kick?"

"Well, now that you mention it."

"Unbelievable. And what about Judy Douglas Knauer? Does she know you have another woman on the side?"

"Why would she care?"

"I thought you seduced her into a real estate deal."

"You have a dirty mind. Everything is not about sex. I didn't seduce anybody into anything."

"You weren't having an affair with Judy Douglas Knauer?"

"Absolutely not."

"So she would have no reason to think you were coming on to her and I stood in her way?"

"Good Lord, no. Why would she think that?"

"I have no idea."

"But *you* think that?"

"I don't think that. I'm just trying to make sense of it all."

"It seems like you're making less and less sense all the time. You're all stressed out. Relax. Take it easy."

Melvin smiled impishly. "Do a crossword."

CHAPTER 59

Judy Douglas Knauer smiled up at Becky Baldwin from her desk in the real estate office. "I've been expecting you."

"I suppose it was inevitable."

"I hope Cora understands how sorry I am."

"I'm not sure she does."

"It is a homicide, after all."

"And you think Cora did it?"

"Don't be silly. I think she was snooping around, trying to figure it out ahead of the police."

"You think that's what she was doing?"

"So that was her I saw."

"You're not sure?"

"I know you can make me look stupid on the witness stand, but just between you and me, it was her. She drove up to the Country Kitchen, parked in the parking lot, walked over to Peggy's truck, and opened the driver's-side door."

"And planted the puzzle?"

"I never said that. I saw her open the door. I saw her reach into the car. It was easy to see, because when she opened the door the overhead light in the cab of the truck came on. She did something on the front seat, exactly what I couldn't say. Then she closed the door, got back in her car, and drove off."

"When she closed the door of the truck, did she have anything in her hand?"

"Her purse. You know, that drawstring thing she carries. What she may or may not have taken out of her purse while it was below my line of sight on the front seat, I couldn't say."

"Uh huh. What about Melvin Crabtree?"

"Who?"

"The defendant. He works for you."

"Oh. Him. He doesn't really work for me. He picked up a few brochures, asked me if he managed to move a house if he could keep whatever he got over the list price as a finder's fee. I said sure, but I didn't expect much. He hasn't sold any. He hasn't *shown* any, either, at least on the inside. He'd have to get a key. At least I hope he would."

"He ever made any advances at you?"

"Not that I noticed."

"Not even a subtle hint?"

"He's not around much. I've got a young

man helping me, doing some actual work. Johnny Dawson. He's got keys, shows houses. Nothing sold yet, but he's got potential."

"Has he now?"

Judy frowned. "Was that catty?" her eyes widened. "Oh, for goodness' sakes. Melvin is Cora's ex. Has she been getting the wrong idea?"

"With Melvin, any idea is the wrong idea."

"She's barking up the wrong tree." Judy sighed. "Poor, Cora."

CHAPTER 60

"Very well," Judge Hobbs said. "Defendant is released on ten thousand dollars bail."

"I have it here, Your Honor," Becky said.

Cora squeezed Becky's arm hard. "If I find out you got that from Melvin," she whispered.

"Try not to maim me till we get outside."

"I mean it, Becky. If it's his money, I won't go."

"Your niece posted bail. And a good thing, too. I can't have all my clients in jail. Just hang on till we get outside."

Rick Reed was waiting to pounce.

"Maybe hang on a little longer," Becky said.

"Cora Felton, is it true you've been arrested trying to free your ex-husband?"

"Just keep walking," Becky said.

Cora broke free. "Yeah, Rick. I staged a jailbreak. I baked a file inside a pie."

"It's no laughing matter. This is a very

serious charge."

"Don't I know it, Rick. Have you ever tasted my cooking? That pie poisoned the whole cellblock."

Becky pulled Cora away. "Must you?"

"Rick Reed brings out the worst in me."

"Melvin doesn't do a bad job, either."

"What's that supposed to mean?"

"Can you wait till we're alone?"

Becky hustled Cora up to her office.

"Okay," Becky said. "If you want to say something stupid, here's the place."

"I don't want to say something stupid. I just want to figure this out."

"I'm glad to hear it. You can start off by leveling with your lawyer."

"What are you talking about?"

"I'm talking about the Melvin factor." Becky put up her hand before Cora could bite her head off. "No, I don't want to hear it. That's the whole problem. Everything about this case is Melvin, Melvin, Melvin. And I don't believe it's because he's guilty, and I don't believe it's because you're trying to protect him. I mean the rest of this nonsense. I want to put that aside and pretend it doesn't exist and look at this crime rationally. The police arrest you for planting evidence in Peggy Dawson's truck. A witness saw you do it. That witness is Judy

Douglas Knauer. You immediately jump to the conclusion she's trying to frame you because she's having an affair with Melvin. You take it for granted, even though you know she probably *did* see you planting evidence in Peggy Dawson's truck."

Cora opened her mouth.

"No, no, I'm not done. I'm a pretty good judge of witnesses. And from talking to Judy Douglas Knauer, two things are abundantly clear. She's not having an affair with Melvin, and she saw you do something with Peggy Dawson's truck. It didn't have to be planting evidence — though how you'll convince me of that when you already expressed the desire to do so I don't know — but you did something, she saw it, and that's how we're in this mess."

Cora blew out a breath. "I stopped at the Country Kitchen, I looked in Peggy Dawson's truck, I realized it was a bad idea, and I didn't do anything."

"You want me to believe that?"

"It's the truth."

"I bet it's not the whole truth."

"Well, if you want to be picky."

"Cora."

"He really wasn't having an affair with Judy Douglas Knauer?"

"He wasn't working for her, either. He

never asked for keys, he's never shown a house."

"That son of a bitch."

"Why would he say he was?"

"So he'd have a reason to be here. When in fact he's merely getting material for his book."

"You should consider making a deal with him. Half the royalties for an acquittal." Becky's eyes widened. "You didn't, did you? Tell me that's not what this puzzle is all about."

"There's going to be another homicide in a minute."

"I'm just saying."

"I don't know who framed Melvin. I don't know who constructed the puzzle. I don't know who planted it in Peggy Dawson's truck. I don't even know who stole the puzzle from Peggy Dawson in the first place. That's where this all starts. With the pur-loined puzzle. Back before anyone was dead. For some reason or other, someone or other wanted me involved in this crime."

Cora smiled, spread her hands. "Well, they certainly got their wish."

Chapter 61

Cora got home to find her niece sunbathing on the front lawn.

"Oh, good, you're out of jail," Sherry said.

"Auntie Cora's out of jail!" Jennifer whooped, turning cartwheels on the lawn.

"She's going to be a big hit at show-and-tell," Cora said.

"One of the perks of having a famous relative."

"I hear you put up bail."

"It seemed the least I could do. I wrote a check on the Puzzle Lady account."

"I'm glad I gave you power of attorney."

"That was nice of you, allowing me to share the fruit of your labor. Your bridge partner turned you in?"

"It was her civic duty."

"No hard feelings?"

"How could there be? Her mind was clouded by Melvin."

"Are you serious?"

"No. According to Becky, she barely knows who he is. Which makes sense. Apparently he dropped by the real estate office and picked up enough knowledge to bluff an unofficial working relationship to give him cover for being in town."

"He really is slimy, isn't he?"

"Hey, that's my ex-husband you're talking about."

"Auntie Cora," Jennifer said brightly. "Did you do a perp walk?"

"What are you teaching her?"

"Some of the lingo. I don't want her to seem uneducated at show-and-tell." Sherry smiled. "Well, I got something for you. I hope it helps."

"What's that?"

"I solved the puzzle."

Cora blinked. "There's another puzzle?"

"No, I solved the one we got."

"What the hell are you talking about?"

"The one with the nonsense rhyme. I figured it out. I feel like a fool for not solving it before."

"You solved it before."

"Yes and no."

"Sherry."

"I solved the nonsense rhyme. I know what it means."

"How did you do that?"

317

"Putting it aside and coming back to it. Things look different with a fresh start."

"All right, what does it mean?"

"Brother."

"What?"

"It means brother. See for yourself." Sherry quoted the puzzle:

"IF NOTHING
IS A BOTHER
ADD ONE ARE
GO FARTHER.

" 'Are' equals 'r.' You add the 'r' to 'bother' and you get 'brother.' How about that? It's not enough the puzzle gives you Johnny Dawson's license plate number. It also says 'brother.' "

"Peggy Dawson's brother?"

"Why not? She's the one with the purloined puzzle."

"My head is coming off."

"Yeah. That's the way with jailbirds. Takes awhile to adjust to society."

"I have to rethink everything."

"Is that bad?"

"What do you mean?"

"Well, nothing you thought of was working. Starting over's not a bad idea."

"You're having too much fun with this."

"I'm not the only one. Aaron's having a ball. He finally got something he can write. It may be the arrest of a family member, but it's from an outside source. He's got the inside scoop on an outside story. It's the best of all possible worlds."

"Glad I could help."

CHAPTER 62

Chief Harper's mouth fell open. "What are you doing here?"

"I thought we should have a little talk," Cora said.

"I can't talk to you. You're a suspect, you've been charged, you're out on bail."

"Thanks for the update, but I actually remembered that."

"Then you ought to know why I can't talk to you. Particularly outside the presence of your attorney. I could contaminate the case. Henry Firth would have a fit."

"Really? Let's get him over here. See what he says."

"I'm not calling the county prosecutor."

"Why not? It's a win-win. You didn't ask me anything. You didn't contaminate anything. The minute I showed up you called him and asked him what he wanted you to do."

"I know what he wants me to do."

"Yeah, but let him tell you. Get it on the record. Or don't call him, and you can explain why you let me hang out in the police station without my lawyer and you didn't do anything about it."

Harper made the call. Whether Henry Firth appreciated it or not, he was there in five minutes.

"What do you think you're doing?" he demanded.

"Ah, you *want* me to talk?" Cora said. "That's a refreshing change. Do I understand you're asking me questions outside the presence of my lawyer, and you want me to answer?"

"If you answer a single question and then try to show malfeasance on my part, I will expose your action for the hollow sham it is. Chief Harper is my witness. The only question you've been asked is why you insist on this meeting that you yourself instigated."

"Works for me," Cora said. "Does that work for you, Chief? You're going to tell the world that I'm a conniving woman who manipulated the police and the prosecutor into contaminating the evidence in order to beat the rap. If we're all happy with that, let's have a little talk. If you're not happy with that, just shut up and listen to what I have to say. Because I'm tired of this case dragging on while you tiptoe around all the legal niceties.

"Okay, here's the deal. Someone framed Johnny and someone framed Melvin. Uh uh! Don't say anything. If you say something, this becomes a discussion, and you don't want that. Just keep quiet. It doesn't mean you agree. There's no reason to proclaim your dissention.

"Where was I? Oh, yes. People framing people. Someone framed Melvin, someone framed Johnny. Obviously it's not the same person — what would be the point? You frame Melvin to get Johnny off the hook. You frame Johnny to get Melvin off the hook.

"Or so one might think. There is the other possibility. You frame Johnny to get Johnny *on* the hook. You frame Melvin to get *Melvin* on the hook.

"That's pretty hard to sort out with two separate framers. It's only slightly better than one."

"What are you talking about?" Henry Firth said.

"Couldn't help yourself, could you?" Cora shook her head. "All right, I'm going to pretend you didn't say that. All open and aboveboard. Chief Harper, please make

322

note of the fact the county prosecutor Henry Firth didn't really ask me that, it was an involuntary exclamation.

"If I may continue. You guys automatically assume I'm responsible for anything that helps Melvin. I have the advantage of knowing I'm not responsible for any of the evidence that helps Melvin. That means someone else is, and that's very interesting, because I can't think of anyone who'd want to help Melvin. It's not just because I was married to him. But it does color my judgment. Because helping Melvin is a concept I can't quite understand.

"Anyway, the evidence that helps Melvin comes in the form of crossword puzzles. The evidence that implicates him comes in the form of physical evidence and eyewitness testimony. This is unfortunate, not just because it implicates me, but because it clouds the picture. Particularly for you guys who start at a disadvantage. But look at it from my point of view.

"There I am, minding my own business. A girl brings me a crossword puzzle, and the next thing I know two people are dead and I'm in jail. That hardly seems fair, does it? Don't worry, that wasn't an attempt to draw you in, you don't have to answer.

"Anyway, you got two suspects. Melvin

and Johnny. Arrested them both, as I recall. So who's the real suspect? Gotta be Johnny. Johnny was arrested first, the puzzle points to him.

"Is there anything to contradict that theory? Only the fact the puzzle that points to him wasn't discovered until after Melvin was arrested. Melvin was arrested, and Johnny was released. Then we get a puzzle implicating Johnny. Was this a desperate attempt to turn the tables, to say, no, no, you got it right the first time?

"And why would someone do that?

"Both of the victims were members of the construction crew. I've heard rumors the construction crew is linked to drugs. The police haven't pursued those rumors because they already have a suspect in jail. Melvin's arrest was pretty convenient for the workers on the construction crew. And who saw Melvin put the damning evidence in his car? A member of the construction crew. It's going to be mighty embarrassing when Becky gets the police on the stand and they admit they haven't even looked into it."

Cora shrugged. "Just a hint.

"For your information, Johnny Dawson stopped by the construction site to tell the guys to stay away from his sister. She's sixteen, by the way, not that it seems to stop her. Anyway, when you couple that with rumors of drug use, it paints a pretty interesting picture."

Cora put her hand over her mouth. "Oh. Did I just give you a motive for Johnny Dawson? I hope not. I wouldn't want to be accused of slanting the evidence to get Melvin out."

Henry Firth frowned.

"Anyway, would you please tell Judy it doesn't matter in the least what she may or may not have seen me do? I know what I did, and that's all that matters, because you guys aren't playing with a full deck anyway. But not having planted a puzzle on Peggy Dawson, the field of suspects is rather thin. Peggy wouldn't do it because it implicates Johnny. The ones with the motive are the boys on the construction crew, and I would say the odds of them coming up with a puzzle range from slim to none. That's just prejudice on my part; they might be geniuses, but I tend to doubt it. But were they capable of it, they're your best bet.

"You with me so far? Once again, don't answer that.

"Now then, I'm sure I can prove myself innocent of all charges in the event of a trial, but I don't intend to let it go that far. I mean to solve this thing. When I do, I'll let you know. I'm not sure how long it will take, because I don't know how many roadblocks you're going to throw in my path. But I'll get there."

Cora nodded in agreement with herself. She smiled, raised her hand.

"Incidentally, Harvey missed something. The nonsense poem about it being a bother? The word 'are' equals the letter 'r.' You add it to 'bother' and get 'brother.' "

Cora ducked out the door of the police station and walked down the street to the *Bakerhaven Gazette.*

Aaron Grant was hard at work typing his story.

"Good news, Aaron. You got an exclusive. The police are investigating drug use on the construction crew, and Peggy's poem spells 'brother.' "

CHAPTER 63

It was funny watching Rick Reed fall all over himself trying to catch up with the exclusive the *Bakerhaven Gazette* had rushed into print. No one was eager to be interviewed, but he managed to snag his buddy Dan Finley, who knew virtually nothing about it.

That made two of them. There was nothing in Rick Reed's report you couldn't get from reading the article except for wild speculation. It was like watching a man drowning.

"Boy, this is fun," Aaron said in between bites.

The family was having dinner in the living room in front of the TV. Sherry had whipped up a new recipe, and the gourmets were sampling.

"I'm glad you're enjoying it," Cora said. "Anytime I can get arrested to help you out, just say the word."

"That's not exactly what I meant," Aaron said.

"Don't let her rain on your parade," Sherry said. "Cora's enjoying it as much as you are."

"That's hardly possible," Aaron said. "Though it sure is nice watching Rick Reed flounder."

"Are the police actually investigating drug use on the construction crew?" Sherry said.

"They have to now. They're not about to deny the report and have people ask why not." Cora speared a forkful. "What are we eating, by the way?"

"What do you mean, what are we eating?"

"I know it's food, I just don't recognize it."

"Wow! You don't get praise like that every day."

"Whatever it is, it's very good. It's just not one of the essential food groups."

"What are the essential food groups?" Aaron said.

"Tacos, burgers, and ice cream."

"I'm afraid none of those are represented," Sherry said. "We're having swordfish, fennel, and risotto."

"We are?"

"If you don't believe me, just ask Aaron."

"Yes, it is," Aaron said.

"Yes, it is what?"

"Whatever she said."

Channel 8 had cut back to the studio, where the news anchors were doing their best not to comment on how uninformative their own report had been. They had just begun to segue into parking problems in Hartford when the picture cut back to Rick Reed. Dan Finley was gone, and Chief Harper had taken his place.

"This is Rick Reed, live, at the police station in Bakerhaven. I'm talking to Chief Harper, who is spearheading the investigation into the murders. Chief Harper, do I understand there has been a break in the case?"

"I wouldn't call it a break, Rick, just a development, and one we thoroughly anticipated. But it's nice to have it confirmed. The tests on the knife found in the glove compartment of suspect Melvin Crabtree's car have been completed."

"That's the knife Jason Tripp observed the suspect himself placing there?"

"Jason Tripp is dead, Rick, and can't speak for himself. Let's just say it's the knife the police recovered after being alerted by Mr. Tripp."

"When you say dead, you mean Mr. Tripp has been murdered."

"The death was ruled a homicide, but that's not the point. We now have the results of the tests performed on the knife."

"And what do the tests show?"

"It's a match. The blood on the knife came from the victim, Fred Winkler."

CHAPTER 64

Cora Felton sat in a booth in the bar at the Country Kitchen. On the table in front of her was a fifth of scotch, a fifth of rum, a fifth of tequila, and a fifth of Knob Creek. She sat, head in hands, staring at the bottles.

Becky Baldwin hurried in the door. The bartender who'd called her pointed to the booth. Becky's mouth fell open. She rushed over, took in the scene.

"Oh, my God!"

Cora said nothing, didn't even acknowledge her presence.

"What are you doing?"

"Thinking."

"And drinking?"

"No."

"What are the bottles?"

"Motivation. These bottles are a forceful reminder of what will happen if I can't solve the case."

"I don't think they have bars in jail."

"They have bars on the cells."

"Why are you so upset? You expected the blood on the knife to be from the victim. Someone framed Melvin with the knife. The knife is the murder weapon. It has the victim's blood. Not a big surprise."

"You sound like I should throw a victory parade."

"You care for him that much?"

Cora lunged to her feet. The bottle of tequila fell over. Becky grabbed it before it rolled off the table.

On the TV over the bar a breaking news banner filled the screen. It gave way to a shot of Rick Reed in front of the police station. The words LIVE, BREAKING NEWS and CHANNEL 8 EXCLUSIVE fought for space along the bottom.

The man standing next to Rick wore a flashy gray suit and a blue striped tie. He reminded Cora of a three-card monte hustler.

"Who is that?" Becky said.

"I have a feeling we're about to find out."

"This is Rick Reed, live, in front of the Bakerhaven police station with a Channel 8 exclusive. I'm talking with Jasper Wasserman, who has some rather startling news regarding the suspect, Melvin Crabtree. Let's get right to it. Mr. Wasserman, what is your relationship to Melvin Crabtree?"

"Melvin is my client."

Becky's mouth fell open. "What!"

"Really?" Rick said. "Are you aware that Rebecca Baldwin is his attorney?"

"So I understand."

"Have you spoken to Miss Baldwin?"

"I have not yet had that pleasure. I certainly intend to."

"Then how can you assume Melvin Crabtree is your client?"

"He hired me."

"I don't understand. How did you contact Mr. Crabtree?"

"He called me from jail. Isn't that something? I must say, it was a first for me."

"You never had a client call you from jail?"

"No."

"You don't take on criminal clients?"

"Not as a general rule."

"Why are you making an exception in this case?"

"Well, it's an exceptional story. I can't wait to talk to him about it."

"You haven't talked to him?"

"Not since I got here. He's in jail."

"Have you asked the police to see him?"

"Yes, I have, and they're not being very cooperative."

"Wait a second. Are you saying the Bakerhaven police are denying you access to your client?"

"That's right."

"On what grounds?"

"On the grounds that Becky Baldwin's his lawyer and she's forbidden him to speak to anybody else."

"Miss Baldwin has forbidden you to approach your client?"

"That's right."

"Why don't you fire her?"

"Why would I do that?"

"Well, if you can't work together, he can't have the two of your fighting over him."

"That's what I said. Melvin doesn't think it's a problem. Of course, he's the one in jail."

"Yes, he is. And how do you intend to get him out of jail?"

"Oh, I don't think I can do that."

"You don't?"

"The police aren't about to let him go. It's a very serious charge. And the second murder is just the icing on the cake. The fact it happened while he was out on bail for the first murder — I couldn't have scripted it better myself."

"Better? It seems to me like your client's in a lot of trouble."

"Oh, I should think so. I understand the

blood on the knife has been shown to have come from the victim. It's like new damning evidence keeps popping up all the time."

"You seem pleased."

"Well, it's not like I bear the man any ill will. And I certainly hope he's exonerated. It just doesn't seem that likely."

"You think he'll be convicted?"

"Certainly not. I'm sure Becky Baldwin is a competent attorney, even if she hasn't let me into her confidence."

Rick Reed frowned. "I don't understand. Are you contesting your rights?"

"Well, I hope it doesn't come to that. I'd like to see Melvin, that's all."

"And there you have it," Rick Reed said. "In an already bizarre murder case, in another stunning development, we now have two attorneys fighting over the defendant. The client has doubtless changed his mind as to his representation, but how can he make his wishes known when he is forced to speak through his attorney?"

Mr. Wasserman raised his hand. "Excuse me. Did you say two attorneys fighting over one client?"

"That's right."

"I'm not an attorney."

Rick Reed blinked. "You're not?"

"Don't be silly. You have to go to law

school. Pass the bar."

"You said Melvin Crabtree was your client."

"Yes, but I'm not his lawyer. I'm his literary agent. I'm representing him in what will surely be a runaway bestseller, *Confessions of a Trophy Husband: My Life with the Puzzle Lady* by Melvin Crabtree."

"Oh, my God!" Cora said.

"What's the matter? You knew this was coming."

"The penny just dropped."

"What are you talking about?"

"I know who framed Roger Rabbit."

CHAPTER 65

Cora skidded to a stop at the top of the driveway, spewing gravel on the lawn. She got a shovel from the toolshed, went out back to the grove of pines, and dug up the takeout container. It was easy in the daylight. She took it inside, sat down at the computer in the office, and Googled New York City laundries. The name of a cleaner on the Upper East Side rang a bell. She picked up the phone, gave them a call.

"Hi. I'm doing my bookkeeping, just came up with an old, unpaid bill. If it's on my account, I'll drop by and pay it off. Can you tell me if it is? The number on the account is two three two eight three seven four. Can you check the account? I'll hold."

Cora was on hold for several minutes. She figured she'd struck out. Then the person came back on the line. "What's that? Melvin Crabtree? Yeah, that's it. Next time I'm in the neighborhood I'll swing by."

Cora put the handkerchief back in the container, thrust the container into her floppy drawstring purse. She hopped in her car and drove out to the real estate office.

Judy wasn't surprised to see her.

"I hope there's no hard feelings."

"Don't be silly," Cora said. "You actually helped me considerably."

"You're kidding."

"Not at all. This case is very confusing, and anything that clarifies the facts is a help."

"Yes, but *you* know what *you* did."

"In this case, not all the time."

Johnny Dawson came in. He ignored Cora and flopped his briefcase onto one of the other desks. "I'm showing the house on Clemson," he said. "Anything you want me to stress?"

"Closet space," Judy said. "The closets are unusually large, and there's quite a few. Keep directing their attention to the inside of the house and away from the fact there's no view."

"Remind me not to buy a house from you," Cora said.

"You already did." Judy held up her hand. "This one's important, Johnny. Give me a minute and I'll ride along with you."

"You don't have to do that."

"Humor me."

Cora left Judy and Johnny talking about the property he was about to show and went out to her car. Johnny had parked next to her. Cora pulled the takeout container out of her purse. She popped the passenger-side door on Johnny's car and spread Melvin's handkerchief out on the seat. Then she got in her car and went home.

CHAPTER 66

Becky called an hour later.

"It's all gone to hell."

"Oh, really?"

"Judy Douglas Knauer found a bloody handkerchief on the front seat of Johnny Dawson's car."

"That's great."

"No, it's not. It's a last-ditch desperate effort to frame Johnny Dawson in order to get Melvin out. The police will be coming to see you soon."

"I can't think why."

"Well, for one thing, you were in the parking lot of the real estate agent just before they found it, and it couldn't have been Melvin himself because he's in jail."

"They don't happen to think it might have been Johnny Dawson?"

"Guess again. The police traced the laundry mark on the handkerchief to a dry cleaner in New York City. The handkerchief belongs to Melvin Crabtree."

"Wow. That certainly looks bad for Melvin, doesn't it?"

"You don't need to sound so happy about it. It also looks bad for you."

"I'm not worried. I got a terrific lawyer."

"Cora."

"You think you could get me some time with your client?"

"Not unless hell freezes over."

"Well, that's inconvenient. You got time to draw up a contract?"

"I got nothing but free time. I got two clients I'm defending from felony charges, and a former client suing me for malpractice. It's every lawyer's dream."

"I'll be right over."

"Just ahead of the posse. If you don't show up, I'll know where to look."

Cora was cut off by a peremptory banging on the door. She glanced out the window. There was a police car in the driveway.

"Never mind," she said. "They're here now."

"Do you realize how much trouble you're in?" Henry Firth said.

"You mind if I answer that?" Cora said.

"I'd prefer if you didn't," Becky said.

"Spoilsport. I'm going to answer it anyway. I don't think I am in any trouble. I think I am at long last free as a bird. Aside from being under arrest, of course. That's the only thing that's put a damper on my day."

The prosecutor turned to Becky. "Why is she acting like this?"

"If I had to hazard a guess, I would say she is fed up with the police handling of this case and has decided to wash her hands of the affair until a more logical course of action is taken."

"What about the charge of planting evidence?"

"I won't have a legal opinion until I've conferred with my client, which I haven't had a chance to do yet. However, she doesn't seem too concerned about it, so I'm just trying to stay out of her way. After all, there's a book agent in town, and I don't really want her writing a tell-all about a small-town lawyer."

"Now there's an idea," Cora said.

"So why don't you ask your questions, and if anything looks too damning, I'll throw myself under the bus."

"I'm not going to answer questions," Cora said. "Becky's concerned enough about growing old without my adding worry lines to her face. But I'm going to talk for a bit, and if anything rings a bell, you might want to make a note.

"A bloody handkerchief is found in Johnny Dawson's car. You immediately assume it's planted. A bloody knife is found in Melvin's car. You immediately assume it's his."

"The handkerchief had Melvin's laundry mark," Henry Firth pointed out.

"Couldn't help yourself, could you? Of course it had Melvin's laundry mark. Otherwise it wouldn't be a good plant.

"The question now is, are the clues real or bogus? The answer is, as you've just pointed out, a little of both. The clues are grounded in reality but not real.

"The same thing with the puzzles. They

get attributed to me, though you know that isn't true. The first puzzle arrived before anyone was killed. Who was I trying to protect Melvin from then? I didn't even know he was in town.

"The fact is, this latest clue you have doesn't pass the smell test. You can only link it to me by implication. I used to be married to the man, therefore I had his handkerchief. I went out to see Judy Douglas Knauer, therefore I had his handkerchief. He's been charged with the crime, therefore I had his handkerchief. The handkerchief had the blood of the victim, therefore I had his handkerchief."

"How do you know it's the victim's blood?"

"If it isn't, what are we talking about? Are you accusing me of planting a totally *irrelevant* handkerchief in Johnny Dawson's car?"

Henry Firth frowned.

Cora pressed her advantage. "This handkerchief is very bad news for you. Because you're the one who has to explain it. Did I plant it in Johnny Dawson's car to frame Johnny Dawson? Did I plant it in Johnny Dawson's car to frame Melvin? Did I plant it in Johnny Dawson's car not realizing it was Melvin's? How is that possible? In that case, where did I get it?

"I'm not explaining any of these things. You have to figure out what you're accusing me of? What *are* you accusing me of? Do you even have a clue?"

Cora chuckled and shook her head. "Boy. Wouldn't like to be in your shoes right now."

CHAPTER 68

"All right," Cora said, "let's draw up that contract."

"What contract?" Becky said.

"The contract with Melvin."

"Melvin won't honor a contract."

"That's why you have to make it legally binding."

"Melvin won't care."

"No, but his publisher will."

Becky frowned. "What are you talking about?"

"I have to tell you something."

"What's that?"

"You know that I can't solve crossword puzzles?"

"Of course I do. That's the reason we have Harvey Beerbaum in our lives."

"I can't construct them either."

"No kidding."

"No, I really can't. Sherry does all the constructing. I just put my name on the —"

Cora broke off, looked at Becky. "How did you mean that?"

"Cora, I'm a lawyer. Did you really think I couldn't figure out you weren't doing the crossword puzzles? Particularly after you admitted you couldn't solve them."

"You knew?"

"Yes."

"And you didn't let on."

"I'm a lawyer. And a friend."

"Do you know how that makes me feel?"

"No, how does it make you feel?"

"Stupid."

"Welcome to the club."

"What club? You knew. You were playing me."

"Instead of the other way around."

"Well, when you put it that way."

"Cora. This is no big deal. If you wanna pretend you're an opera singer, I bet you could bluff your way through it. The only one who could possibly care is Granville Grains, and I'm already preparing your legal defenses in case they find out and are pissed. There's two murder charges against Melvin and God knows how many charges against you. And I'd kind of like to deal with them first."

"Fine," Cora said. "So hone your legal

mind, grab a pencil, and let's bang out that contract."

Chapter 69

Cora drove out to the real estate agency, but Johnny Dawson had just left. She caught him on Holcomb Lane, pulled alongside at the overpass, and ran him off the road.

He came up madder than a wet hen. "Keep away from me or I'll call the cops."

"Call 'em if you like. You got nothing to fear from me. I know you think I'm out to get you. I'm trying to solve a murder. Just between you and me, I don't think you did it. If you don't think you did it, then we concur, there's no reason we shouldn't get along."

"What do you want?"

"That's the spirit. That's the attitude that's going to get you through this. All I want's a little conversation. It didn't used to be so hard to get a man to talk to me. I guess I'm losing my charm."

Johnny snorted angrily. "I'm outta here."

Cora put up her hands. "Sorry. I'll stop talking about me. Let's talk about you. You're an army man, right? You were in Iraq?"

"Afghanistan."

"How many tours of duty?"

"Three."

"Lose many buddies?"

"What do you think?"

"Take a lot of drugs? Odds are you did. Three tours of duty. I'll bet you got hooked pretty bad. You come back home, your parents are dead, your sister's your ward. You ship out she's a skinny tomboy; you come back she's Courtney Love. No surprise you'd go nuts. Particularly with the drugs. You've seen what drugs can do. Here's your innocent little sister hanging out with construction workers who want to get her high and get into her pants. No wonder you'd want to kill them."

"I didn't kill anyone."

"I know. You know how I know? A crossword puzzle said you did. And crossword puzzles lie. It's in their nature. Nine times out of ten a crossword puzzle tells you something, it's a load of crap. Did you threaten those guys? I know you did after the murders, but I'll bet you did it before. They were real druggies, weren't they?

350

Messing around with your sister. It's hard to imagine you *not* killing them."

"I thought you were on my side."

"I am, but the facts are the facts. These guys represented access to a considerable quantity of dope. Your sister wanted that dope. You didn't want her to have it. On that we both agree."

"I didn't agree to anything."

"No, but let's say you did. Just for the sake of argument. Both of the victims, you warned them off your sister, didn't you? You told them to leave her alone. Threatened them if they didn't. I would say that threat led directly to their death."

"But you're on my side," Johnny said sarcastically. "You don't think I killed anybody."

"Johnny, I know you didn't. At least I don't think so. But it's a little hard to demonstrate with all the constraints that have been placed on me. I've been arrested. I'm out on bail. You've been arrested, but you got released pretty quick when the cops got someone better. So you got nothing to gripe about. For a guy who looked so incredibly guilty, you came out smelling like a rose. And I'm beginning to think I know why."

"Why?"

"Because you're out of your league. You're in the game with master manipulators, and it turned out it's more convenient for you to be innocent."

"Now you're just talking weird."

"I know. But do me a favor. Not that you owe me one. And not because you necessarily appreciate what I'm doing. But just because it's the right thing to do."

"What do you want?"

"Did you threaten Fred Winkler and Jason Tripp?"

"Are you wearing a wire?"

Cora chuckled, shook her head. "Oh, God, if you could only search me. But you're much too young. No, I'm not wearing a wire. Not that it matters. A bloody murder weapon trumps a few idle threats any day of the week. No, I'm not attempting to entrap you. I'd just like to know if you did. Just between us, did you threaten those two guys?"

"I'd rather not say."

"No matter. I'm like the media. No comment's as good as a yes. So tell me something else. Why didn't you want us to search your room?"

Johnny was startled by the sudden change of subject. "What?"

"I thought it was because you found your

352

sister's puzzle in your room and you didn't want us to think you stole it, but that wasn't it, was it?"

Johnny couldn't meet her eyes.

"You backslid, didn't you? You're lecturing your sister about drug use, and you've got a stash in your room. Probably just pot, which wouldn't be a big deal if you weren't a big brother. So you couldn't let us search your room.

"And to make matters worse, you *had* found your sister's puzzle in your room, so you trashed it. And turned in a bloody knife. You took an old hunting knife, and you cut yourself, arm, leg, somewhere it wouldn't show, and you called the cops and told 'em you'd found it under your pillow. To confuse the issue and account for not wanting your room searched. A delicate balancing act, but you pulled it off.

"Except you gave the killer ideas. Knock someone off with a hunting knife, you'll probably get the blame. Which is how you got arrested. The flimsiest possible frame, it couldn't possibly work, there had to be more to it. But before there was, a better suspect turned up.

"Anyway, that's how it all started, and that's how we got into this mess. And now it's out of control. And I'm gonna try to

353

clean it up."

Johnny stood defiantly, admitting nothing.

Cora put her hand on his shoulder, smiled ruefully. "Try not to hate me too much."

CHAPTER 70

Cora drove down to the police station.

"Fit me with a wire."

Chief Harper was startled. "Why?"

"Johnny Dawson asked me if I was wearing one. It seemed like a good idea."

"You're going to talk to Melvin with a wire?"

"There's an idea. But I don't think so. If I talked to Melvin with a wire for ten minutes you could probably indict us both."

"Who's it for?"

"I'll let you know if it works."

"If it doesn't, you won't?"

"Much as I know you glory in my failures, I'd just as soon keep this one under wraps."

"Am I going to be happy if it works?"

"Define happy."

"Cora."

"You'll catch a killer. It may not be the one you want."

"You really are exasperating."

"You're stalling. Could it be the Baker-haven police don't *have* a wire?"

"We have a wire. I'm considering the logistics."

"Logistics?"

"Ordinarily you'd have a female officer wire you up, but we don't happen to have a female officer."

"And don't you think *that's* way overdue?"

"I don't want to fight that fight right now. I've got enough problems to deal with."

"Like seeing me naked?"

"That's not going to be an issue. I'll show you where it should go and you can change in the bathroom."

"Spoilsport."

"You are going to let us *hear* this recording, aren't you?" Harper said ironically.

"If it's any good."

"I'll be the judge of that."

"Okay. On one condition."

"What's that?"

"If I get what you need, you let me talk to Melvin."

"With a wire?"

"No. Alone."

"If you get what we need, Melvin will be released."

"No. You let me talk to him first. And you hold the arrest until I do."

356

"That may be a deal breaker."

"Then I won't tell you what I get. Becky can talk to Melvin, and I'll decide if we want to share."

Harper shook his head. "Then you don't get a wire."

"So I'll buy a digital at Staples, wire myself, and take all the credit. I can't see Henry Firth being too happy at that."

"You think you know what happened?"

"Not everything. But I think I know who did it."

"In your version it wasn't Melvin."

"That's what I'd like to determine."

"But you think you know."

"I have a theory I'd like to test by wearing a wire. I don't have to, but that's the way it helps you."

"You are so infuriating."

"Thank you."

Chief Harper sighed. "Okay, if you get the goods, I'll hold the arrest until you speak to Melvin."

"Deal."

Harper pressed the intercom. "Dan. Set Cora up with a wire."

CHAPTER 71

Peggy's truck was parked out at the construction site. The girl herself was wrapped around the neck of one of the crew. Cora recognized him as the guy she had asked when the shift ended. He seemed torn between the forbidden fruit and the evil eye of the foreman urging him back to work. From the way Peggy kept pleading and showing her watch, Cora figured it must be near the end of the shift.

The foreman won out. Peggy huffed on the sideline while her prey headed back to the building under construction and climbed up into the girders. Peggy paced up and down impatiently.

"Jonesing, are you?" Cora said

Peggy looked up startled. "What?"

"Can't wait for your next fix. Or hit. Or toke. Or whatever they call it with crack, or freebase, or whatever they call however they're doing cocaine these days. You shooting it yet? I don't see any marks on your arms, but then you're young."

"I don't know what you're talking about."

"Of course not. Because I'm an old hippie, and you're a perennial millennial. You must have read in the paper that I figured out the puzzles. Well, you probably didn't read it in the paper, but maybe you saw it on TV. Bother is brother, and your brother's license plate number is in play.

"Of course that was the second puzzle. The first puzzle was a noncommittal did he do it? Which bothered me for a while. Before I remembered that the first puzzle was stolen and only found later."

Peggy said nothing, continued to fidget.

"You ever see the movie *The Bad Seed*? Of course not. You're much too young. It was in black and white, for goodness' sakes. Patty McCormack was this sweet little girl. Blond hair, pigtails, cutest little thing. Well, she kills people. Later in the movie it turns out she was adopted and her real mother was actually a criminal. The Bad Seed, you see. It's quite a movie. Scary as hell. Except for the end. They tacked on a last scene where her mother puts her across her knee and spanks her. It's like a ha-ha-we-were-only-kidding scene to let the audience go home feeling good. Total cop-out. I hated it, of course. Anyway, that's *The Bad Seed.*"

"So?"

"You weren't adopted, were you? You had a genuine mother and father. Lived with them in the City up until last year when they had a little accident. Drove their car off the road."

Cora put her arm around Peggy's shoulders, leaned in confidentially as if she were the director coaching a young starlet. "This is the part in the movie where you say in a voice that's positively chilling, 'It wasn't an accident. I cut their brake lining.'"

"What are you talking about?"

"I'm auditioning you for the role. Trying to see how well you'd do. I'm afraid you're not that bad."

"You're acting really weird."

"That's what Johnny said. Must run in the family." Cora chuckled. "He must have been a real shock, wasn't he? Tough soldier, back from the wars. You figured he'd be your buddy. You figured he'd be on your side. Big shock when he doesn't want to do drugs. Instead he wants to keep you away from the guys who do. Mom and Dad were bad, but they were squares. They had no idea what was going on. Johnny's hip and won't play games. You can't wrap him around your finger. He's a huge wet blanket.

I mean, here you are, acting like a grown woman, and here's big brother, treating you like a naughty child, grounding you and cutting off your allowance.

"Could it be worse? I don't think so. You like drugs, you're being cut off. You like boys, you're being cut off. You can sneak out and meet 'em in the middle of the night, but that's schoolgirl games. Just the image you want to avoid.

"What you really need are some drugs to tide you over until the humiliation stops.

"And that's when you started making crossword puzzles."

"I never made any puzzles."

"Yeah, you did. You made one and you told me about it. But you didn't bring it with you, that was the interesting thing. You would think, if you were hoping to meet me and ask me to do a puzzle, that you'd have the puzzle. At the time I didn't wonder why, I was just delighted you didn't. It made it easier to palm you off on Harvey Beerbaum.

"But a funny thing happened on the way to the puzzle. It disappeared. Someone stole it. The Purloined Puzzle. I'm sure it was supposed to show up in Johnny's possession, but before it could, something else did.

"A bloody knife. Which made no sense to anyone since it showed up a day before the

361

murder.

"And that's where the comedy of errors begins.

"In most cases, A triggers B and B triggers C. In this case, B triggers A and . . . Well, I can't sort it all out in the abstract, my head would come off. So let's go back to real life.

"You made up a puzzle and you wanted me to find it and solve it."

Cora put up her hand. "Don't protest. Otherwise you'll be protesting all afternoon, and you'll never get your drugs. You made up the puzzle. You wanted me to find it and solve it. More to the point, you wanted me to find it and solve it after your brother had apparently tried to suppress it.

"Only Johnny wouldn't play along. When the cops wanted to search his room, he wouldn't allow it, and before they could get a warrant he voluntarily surrendered a bloody hunting knife he claimed he found planted under his pillow.

"Well, you didn't plant that knife."

"Thank you," Peggy said sarcastically.

"But it gave you ideas. Johnny's got a bloody knife. Suppose someone were killed with the knife? Suppose someone Johnny *didn't like* were killed with that knife? Specifically the guy who'd been giving you drugs?"

"Yeah, like I'd really want to kill him."

"Well, let's examine that," Cora said. "The downside is you lose a drug-dealing boyfriend. On the plus side, you rip off his stash. And you frame your brother, who'd become a real pain in the ass, for murder."

"And then I undermine all my good work by planting the actual murder weapon in some other guy's car."

"Of course not. You didn't do that. And you were shocked when you heard someone did. That can't be the murder weapon. You've *got* the murder weapon. What the hell is another knife doing in the equation? It simply makes no sense. You gotta admit, for your first murder things are going *unusually* wrong. Here you had your brother neatly framed for the murder, and some interloper crashes the party. Where the hell did he come from? You were just about to spring the puzzle accusing your brother, and suddenly he's not the suspect anymore. Talk about reversals of fortune.

"Luckily, you haven't turned in the crossword puzzle yet. You have time to whip up a new one. And what is it? A message casting doubt on the guilt of the current suspect. I don't know who this guy Melvin is, but he certainly didn't do it. Which you know all too well. You turn in that one, saving the brother one for when you get the focus back on him.

"Only it doesn't happen. Melvin's too good a suspect. He's got your brother beat all to hell. The cops focus on Melvin, and your brother's all but forgotten. In desperation, you play the puzzle card. It's got a cryptic message that says 'brother,' and it points to his license plate number in a Sudoku.

"It still doesn't work. Your brother's the original Teflon man. Nothing sticks to him. Defying all logic, the other guy remains in jail. What the hell is that all about? Why hasn't he fought himself out by now?

"And yet the fact that he hasn't yields a flicker of hope. Being in jail is a perfect alibi. If someone else were killed, Melvin couldn't possibly have done it. And the police would have to look around for somebody else. All you need is another victim who fits the pattern. I would say that young man you had your arms draped around is probably not long for this world. Particularly with your brother bawling out the guys on the crew in front of half a zillion witnesses.

"Meanwhile, this guy just keeps looking guiltier and guiltier. The blood on the knife in his glove compartment came from the victim? How the hell did that happen?

You've got the knife with the victim's blood on it. At least you used to. The police have it now. They just don't know it. They took it out of the back of the second victim. Only it's got so much of his blood on it they can't *find* the first victim's blood. Oh, they could if they looked for it, but that's the last thing they're looking for. And you can't run down to the police station and say, 'Hey, schmuck, it's the same knife, test it for the first guy, too.'

"I suppose if we gave you enough time you could come up with a crossword puzzle that explained it, but it would have to be so complicated that even Will Shortz couldn't solve it with CliffsNotes and a map."

"Will who?"

Cora rolled her eyes. "Oh, *that's* the part that bothers you. You're in trouble, kid. Your brother isn't taking the fall for murder. You probably are, but even if you don't, you're not going to be happy. Because your plan failed, and your brother's going to be as big a pain in the ass as he's ever been. More so, if the guys you hang out with keep getting killed. If you have an overprotective guardian, that's not the way to go."

"How do you know so much?"

"I hardly know anything. I know the guy in jail's innocent. I know your brother's innocent. I know the two dead guys are in-nocent. That doesn't leave much else. If I were you, I'd start binge-watching *Orange Is the New Black*. Bone up on your new life-style."

"I'm underage."

"So you're allowed to kill people? I don't think that's how it works. You want me to look it up? I got a great lawyer. I don't think she'll take your case, but she can tell you what you'll get.

"If you stop now and go to the cops, you might catch a break. If you kill someone else, they'll take a dim view."

"How'd you figure it out?"

"The knife had to be in one of two places. At the bottom of a lake or in the back of the victim. It's more useful to me if it's in the back of the victim, so I decided on that. If I'm wrong, feel free to correct me."

Peggy frowned and fidgeted.

"Anyway, your new man seems nice. For a drug dealer banging a minor. I'd hate to see him get killed for no reason. Trust me, killing him is not going to help you at all. It's not going to reflect on your brother. It might help Melvin, but you don't care about that. You want to get Johnny out of your life. This isn't the way to do it. So do yourself a favor."

Cora cocked her head.
"Don't kill anybody else."

CHAPTER 72

Cora walked into the interrogation room. "Hi, Melvin, how you doing?"

Melvin scowled. "How did you get in here?"

"I made a deal with the cops. If I can make a deal with you, we all win. If I can't, we all lose. I'll lose pretty bad, but you'll lose worst of all."

"Wait a minute. You made a deal with the cops?"

"Tentative. It's all dependent on my coming to terms with you. If I can't do that, the deal is off."

"That makes no sense."

"No, it doesn't. Which is fitting, because nothing about this case really does. There's too many scam artists involved. Not the least of which is you."

"Can I go back to my cell?"

"Of course you can. Just sign this contract first."

368

"What contract?"

"I had Becky draw up a contract to wind this whole thing up. If you sign it, we can get on with our lives. If you don't, well, jail seems to agree with you."

"Let's see the contract."

"We have to solve the crime first."

"*We* have to solve the crime?"

"Yeah. You and me. The original Nick and Nora. We're perfect for the parts. I've even got a little dog."

"You're not amusing me."

"I'm not trying to. Shut up and pay attention. I'll tell you what happened."

"You *know* what happened?"

"More than you do. Let me fill you in." Cora held up her hand, slipped into lecture mode. "Who stole Peggy Dawson's puzzle and who framed you? If I could figure that out, it would be a huge step forward. It still wouldn't solve the crime, but it would clear away some of the deadwood, making the solution obvious. What I was hoping for, what would have been really neat, was if you stole Peggy's puzzle and Peggy framed you. It would have a nice symmetry to it. And you and jailbait is a match made in heaven."

"She's much too young."

"Don't make me laugh, Melvin. You're the

369

original cradle robber. Hell, you've dated sperm."

"That line sounds familiar. Did you use it in the divorce hearing?"

"Let's not get sidetracked. We need to end this fiasco. The way I see it, there are two possible outcomes. One, you go to trial, you get convicted, your book comes out, you make a pile of money, only you can't spend it in jail. Or, two, the police catch the real killer, the case against you is dismissed, your book comes out and makes a small fortune, but not nearly as much as a book by a killer would make. On the other hand, you get to spend every cent because you're a free man. Which plan do you like?"

"Am I supposed to say Plan B?"

"You're supposed to choose whatever brings you true happiness. Freedom and a small fortune sounds good to me, but then it's not my money."

Melvin considered. "I'm not sure taking the rap is as lucrative as the portrait you paint. There's something to be said for the killer who cheated justice."

"Yeah, but it ain't you, babe. You're putting up a brave front, Melvin, but the fact is you're scared. Everything that could possibly go wrong, has. The murder weapon was a clever frame, and I'm afraid it's gonna get you. The only way out is to play ball."

"I'm not following this."

"Of course not. Remember when I said the ideal thing would be if you stole Peggy's puzzle and Peggy framed you? That didn't happen. Turned out it was the other way around. And I never would have got it if it wasn't for your agent. That was a bit of an overreach, and it's coming back to bite you. The minute your agent started plugging the book, I realized what happened.

"*Peggy* stole the puzzle and *you* framed you.

"You hadn't meant to. But when you saw Johnny Dawson marched into the police station with the TV cameras rolling, dollar signs went off in your head. You saw your book suddenly leap from mid-list to best-seller. It's not just confessions of a trophy husband anymore. It's confessions of a murder suspect. With luck, they could rush the book out while you're still on trial.

"So, what do you do? You speed out to Target and buy a hunting knife. You keep the receipt to be able to prove you did. You rush back to the motel and get the bloody handkerchief, the one you used to wipe Fred Winkler's blood off your hands. It's not from the murder. It's from the fistfight. When you punched him in the face and

371

gave him a bloody nose. You stain the knife with enough blood that forensics will be able to prove that it's his.

"You wait in your motel room until one of the construction workers drives up. It's Jason Tripp, sneaking back to the motel on his lunch hour to do some drugs. You come out of the motel and you stick the knife in your glove compartment when he's sure to notice. Then you drive out to the Country Kitchen for a beer, stopping at a pay phone on the way to give an anonymous tip to the cops to search your car. Jason Tripp didn't phone that tip in, you did. As soon as you were caught with the weapon, he was happy to take credit.

"The cops pick you up, search your car, find the knife. Suddenly Johnny Dawson's off the hook and you're on it. Golden boy. Media darling. The one Rick Reed wants to interview. You go on TV and get interviewed as often as possible, paving the way for your agent to show up and publicize the book. Ignoring your attorney's warning, you blab your guts out. You say anything you want. You don't care, as long as you get the publicity. You're not worried; you've got the sales receipt, proving the knife was bought after the crime.

"Guess what? It's not going to happen.

Because the dramatic piece of evidence you planned on producing to prove your innocence has disappeared. And guess what? I've got it. I can produce it, or I can flush it down the toilet. So let's make a deal. And there's no reason to involve your agent. Or your lawyer, for that matter."

"Wait a minute. You have my receipt?"

"Of course I do. Where'd you think it went?"

"You stole it?"

"That's right. So let's play Deal or No Deal."

"You give me the receipt and I don't write the book?"

"Don't be silly. You've got a contract. You've got to write the book."

"So you want me to go easy."

"Of course not. They'd want their advance back. *Confessions of a Trophy Husband.* You promised them the inside scoop on a scandalous sex life, and that's what you gotta give 'em. Tell 'em every intimate detail. If you can't remember, make it up. I won't contradict you. Have fun. Describe that three-way we never had."

"Well, actually —"

"That wasn't me, you twit! I can understand how you'd get confused. You certainly did when we were married. So lay it on thick. I don't know if Granville Grains will stand behind me. If not, we can revisit your alimony. Your income will have substantially changed."

"So you're going to hold me up."

"That was a joke. I'm not going to say boo, unless you wanna count no comment. You can say absolutely anything you want. Just don't kill the golden goose."

"What are you talking about?"

"Don't out me. That's the centerpiece of your book, right? That I'm a fraud? Well, you don't need that anymore. You got sex and murder. You're one of the few people who know I'm Milli Vanilli. Say so in our book, and the deal is off."

"How?"

Cora shook her head. "See? That's why this is such an iffy proposition. There's nothing to keep you from going back on your word. Except your honor and sense of fair play."

"I can see how that would be a problem."

"So how do we get around it? I'm working on scenarios that automatically recant your alibi evidence in the event of a betrayal, but then you run into double jeopardy and whether it's attached, since a dismissal is not a bar to future prosecution, and the whole thing becomes a horrible mess. I'd like to circumvent that. Hence the contract."

"What is the contract?"

"It's a contract between you and me for an equitable distribution of the royalties from your new book."

"The hell it is. You have no right to any of my royalties."

"Well, that would be one contention. The other is I do. The lawyers fight it out and the judge decides."

"My publisher would not be a party to any such contract."

"Your publisher won't even know. The contract is between you and me. If you're a good boy, no one will ever know. If you're not, everything goes to hell and it's a dogfight. Anyway, here's the contract. You don't have to read it. You're much too angry, and I don't want to put you through it. But I can give you the gist.

"As I said, the contract specifies our agreement on the distribution of the royalties. The math is rather simple. According to the contract, you get one hundred percent of the royalties and I get none."

"What?"

"If that works for you, it works for me. But that's only if you live up to the terms of the contract."

"What terms?"

"Not too tough. All you have to do is agree that you will not in any way imply that I might not be capable of creating crosswords. Should you do that, the original distribution is void, and the second percentages kick in. In that case you get twenty percent of the royalties and I get eighty."

"Are you out of your mind?"

"More than likely, but those are the terms. Sorry to ask for so much, but I want to make something on this deal, and in that event the royalties on the book aren't going to be very high."

Melvin's face darkened. "What do you mean?"

"You out me, I'll out you. You can be the romantic hero, framed for murder. Or you can be the sniveling snake oil salesman just trying to make a buck."

"How do you plan to do that?"

"It's pretty obvious, Melvin. I got your receipt from Target. I can prove you framed yourself."

"Give me a break."

"I am. That's why I'm here, talking to you, instead of the police. I could present them with a solution of the crime, but that wouldn't do any good for either of us.

"I don't think you appreciate the delicacy of the Target receipt. You thought you could

376

have Becky produce it and claim that the killer, having already disposed of the real murder weapon, bought an identical knife to frame you with. And the prosecution wouldn't be calling in the sales clerk from Target to prove you bought the knife, because they'd be proving you bought it after the murder and it had nothing to do with the crime.

"But that's a worst-case scenario. You're probably counting on me to solve the crime. Well, guess what. I'm not going to do it. I can't be bothered. I'm gonna hang on to my clipping and let you fry. Unless the cops are an awful lot brighter than they've shown so far and solve it themselves, and that ain't gonna happen. You'll be convicted on the evidence, the book will make a ton of money, and you'll be in jail.

"My career will be in tatters, but that will be a small consolation knowing I'm not going to lift a finger to get you out."

"You wouldn't do that," Melvin said.

"What? Do nothing? I'm great at doing nothing. My career's over, I got no obligations, there's nothing to keep me. Maybe I'll take a cruise. Or maybe I'll write my own book. *Confessions of a Killer's Wife: My Life with Melvin Crabtree.*

"Or sign this contract and I'll have you out of here by lunch."

CHAPTER 73

Cora came out of the interrogation room holding the signed contract.

"All set?" Chief Harper said.

"Yeah. Thanks for holding off."

"I can pick up Peggy Dawson now?"

"Any time."

"Dan?"

"I'm on it."

Dan Finley went out the door.

"You gonna tell me what that was all about?" Chief Harper said.

"Just getting Melvin to agree."

"Agree to what?"

"Not rock the boat. You want a smooth transition, right? No public ridicule, no charges of false arrest. Melvin's gonna stress the incident as a dramatic vindication of the American judicial system. Any man may be charged, but it takes a jury of one's peers to declare one guilty. There's no stigma attached to being arrested. It will make a wonderful chapter for his book."

"I'm going to look like an idiot."

"You're going to look like a hero. That's why I had you wire me instead of recording the girl with a digital from Best Buy. You're the courageous police officer making sure he was proceeding against the right man. You're going to look damn good."

"And then Henry Firth will take me out to the woodshed."

"That's why you're going to let him stand up and take the credit."

"I suppose," Harper said.

"What's the matter?"

"There's some holes in your story."

"Like what?"

"If Peggy was trying to frame her brother, who framed Melvin?"

Cora spread her arms. "Don't look at me. I know you think it's just the sort of thing that I would do, but trust me, I didn't. I'm sure if I poked around I could find enough people Melvin has ticked off to come up with someone who thought it would be the perfect revenge to frame him, but if he gets out it hardly matters who got him in."

"Doesn't he want to know?"

"If he does, that's just tough. I got him off the hook for murder. If he wants revenge, that's his business. My work is done."

Cora smiled at Chief Harper and, clutching her precious contract, sailed out the door.

CHAPTER 74

"Becky knows I can't do crossword puzzles."

"So?"

"You're not upset?"

"What? That my husband's ex-girlfriend who has always had the edge of being a brilliant trial lawyer is aware of the fact I have a highly skilled expertise of my own?" Sherry shrugged. "I can live with that."

"Well, when you put it that way," Cora said.

"And she's not going to spill the beans?"

"She's my lawyer."

"What about Melvin?"

"He'll be out as soon as they clear up the paperwork."

"What paperwork?"

"Beats me. I don't think there is any. They're not going to let him out until they update Henry Firth. He's the one who's going to have to explain the change of defendants."

"That should be embarrassing."

"Not as embarrassing as it could be."

"No kidding. Henry Firth doesn't suspect?"

"No, and he's not gonna. That and the fact Melvin framed himself. No one's gonna find that out because it would hurt sales of his book."

"You care about his book sales?"

"I care about ours. As long as his book is selling, he isn't going to hurt us. If it flops, he might try to take us down."

"You think it'll happen?"

"Hell, no. His book's gonna sell if I have to go on TV talk shows and admit there's a part of my life I'm not particularly proud of. If I play my cards right, sales on our Puzzle Lady books will go up."

Sherry pointed to the TV. "Here they come."

Melvin and Henry Firth came out the front door of the police station. From the way they acted, they might have been old golfing buddies. Henry wrapped his arm around Melvin's shoulders and faced the camera.

"Mr. Prosecutor," Rick Reed said. "I understand you're releasing Melvin Crabtree from custody. What does this mean?"

"A great miscarriage of justice has been

averted, Rick. And we have the Bakerhaven police force and Chief Harper in particular to thank. Moments ago, Peggy Dawson, faced with irrefutable evidence collected by the police, confessed to the crimes. She and she alone killed Fred Winkler and Jason Tripp. Mr. Crabtree has been exonerated of all charges, and I must say he is being gracious about the confusion that led to his arrest."

"Mr. Crabtree, this must be a huge relief."

"You bet it is, Rick. But I must say I wasn't concerned. I had no doubt that the situation would be cleared up, and that's exactly what happened."

"Can you tell us the circumstances that led to your arrest?"

Melvin smiled. "I could. But you're going to have to wait for my book, *Confessions of a Murder Suspect: My Life with the Puzzle Lady.*"

"Would that be the same book your agent announced as *Confessions of a Trophy Husband?*"

"That was the original title, Rick, but recent events have thrust me center stage. As an innocent man who was nearly tried for two murders I didn't commit, I find myself in the position of being somewhat of a celebrity myself. My publisher's dancing on the ceiling, and my agent's looking for a movie deal."

"You think he'll get a movie deal?" Sherry said.

"Stranger things have happened."

"That might be interesting. I wonder who would play you."

"You name an actress over sixty and I'll break your head."

Sherry suddenly became very interested in the TV screen.

Aaron Grant wandered in. Sherry seized on the chance to change the subject. "You're not covering this?"

"I already filed my stories. Cora gave me a heads-up. I know what they're going to say."

"Then you must be psychic. Rick Reed might say anything."

"True, but it's not newsworthy. Cora gave me everything else." Aaron sank down on the couch, leaned back. "Of course, none of it's exclusive. You got anything exclusive for me, Cora? Anything at all?"

Cora considered. "Well, I got a couple of exclusives, but you can't write 'em."

"That figures. Please tell me it's nothing sensational that will break my heart to sit on."

Cora and Sherry exchanged glances.

"Well," Cora said, "Melvin framed himself for murder and slept with the prosecutor's wife."

Aaron blinked.

"Kill me now."

ABOUT THE AUTHOR

Parnell Hall was presented with the Life Achievement Award by the Private Eye Writers of America at the 2015 Shamus Awards banquet.

Parnell is a former President of the Private Eye Writers of America, and a member of Sisters in Crime. He lives in New York City.

The employees of Thorndike Press hope you have enjoyed this Large Print book. All our Thorndike, Wheeler, and Kennebec Large Print titles are designed for easy reading, and all our books are made to last. Other Thorndike Press Large Print books are available at your library, through selected bookstores, or directly from us.

For information about titles, please call:
  (800) 223-1244

or visit our website at:
  gale.com/thorndike

To share your comments, please write:
  Publisher
  Thorndike Press
  10 Water St., Suite 310
  Waterville, ME 04901

LP 3199

RECEIVED OCT 2 2 2018